THREADS OF TRUTH

PATCHWORK MYSTERIES

THREADS OF TRUTH

KRISTIN ECKHARDT

Guideposts
New York, New York

www.guideposts.com
(800) 932-2145
Guideposts Books & Inspirational Media

Cover design by Wendy Bass
Cover illustration by Joyce Patti
Interior design by Lorie Pagnozzi
Typeset by Aptara

Printed and bound in the United States of America
10 9 8 7 6 5 4 3 2 1

DEDICATION

For my wonderful daughter,

Chelsea Schuyler Eckhardt

PATCHWORK MYSTERIES

THREADS OF TRUTH

 CHAPTER ONE

Sarah Hart leaned forward, squinting to see through the tiny shards of ice clinging to the windshield. She hated driving in icy conditions, especially in unfamiliar territory. Her gloved hands gripped the steering wheel as she drove along the dark country road, looking for some signs of life. She hadn't seen a house for miles, not one place she could stop and ask for directions.

Her twin granddaughters both dozed in the car, Audrey in the bucket seat beside her and Amy in the back, her long legs stretched across the seat. Sarah had asked them to go to Hartford with her after she'd been invited to give a workshop at the annual Connecticut Quilt Makers Conference. They were more excited about spending the weekend in a hotel than about attending the conference, but she would make sure they had fun.

The plan had been to leave Friday evening after Amy's junior high basketball game and arrive at the Red Clover Inn by nine o'clock. Unfortunately, Sarah hadn't planned on encountering an ice storm or getting lost on the way to the historic country inn. The inn was located on the outskirts of Hartford and the map was hard to follow. She'd tried calling the inn for directions, but her cell phone kept cutting out.

Icy sleet and ominous darkness filled the night sky. Sarah tried not to be afraid but it wasn't easy, especially since she still wasn't sure if they were heading in the right direction. She could see the city lights of Hartford glowing on the horizon. The moment she thought she should circle back, her headlights flashed on a white wooden sign with RED CLOVER INN painted in bright red letters.

Finally!

She tried to depress the brakes gently, but the tires skidded on the slick asphalt before the Grand Prix finally came to a stop. She shifted the car into reverse, carefully backed up, and turned into the private driveway that led to the inn.

"Are we there yet?" Amy's groggy voice asked from the backseat. She still wore her royal blue and white jersey under her coat along with a pair of blue flannel pants.

"Yes, we finally made it," Sarah replied as Audrey began to stir beside her. Relief flowed through her as she breathed a silent prayer. *Thank you, Lord, for bringing us here safely.*

Through the towering blue spruce trees lining the long driveway, Sarah glimpsed the shadowy outline of the inn ahead of her. She had heard about the secluded inn from Spencer Hewitt, Maple Hill's librarian, and had been intrigued by its history. According to Spencer, the English-style manor house had been built in 1890, during the height of the Gilded Age, and still retained most of its original décor and period furniture.

Audrey yawned, tugging the hood of her coat back to reveal her long blonde hair in a messy ponytail. She leaned forward for a better view of the inn, her blue eyes surveying the icy landscape with surprise. "This is where we're staying?"

"It sure is," Sarah replied.

The two-story inn constructed of russet sandstone loomed in front of them. The double chimneys stretched like two long arms into the turbulent gray clouds above. Leafless shrubs hugged the front of the house, their naked branches shivering in the wind.

She pulled alongside a line of cars and switched off the engine. The rattle of sleet grew louder. "Let's grab our bags and get inside," Sarah told them. "Just be careful in case the sidewalk is slippery."

Audrey slung her backpack over one shoulder and popped open her car door, admitting a frigid blast of air. "Wow, it's freezing out here!"

Sarah reached for her overnight bag. The twins were almost at the front entrance by the time she locked the car and headed down the sidewalk. She bent her head to shield her face from the wind, the sleet stinging her face. The twins waited for her by the solid oak door, Amy tracing the iron scrollwork over the frosted glass panel with one gloved finger. Sarah turned the brass doorknob and walked inside the grand, two-story foyer, the girls close on her heels.

The warmth of the inn melted away the tension that had gripped Sarah during the long trip. To the left of the foyer was a large parlor filled with antique furniture, beautiful Persian rugs, and a roaring blaze in the stone fireplace. Heavy gold drapes hung from the top of the windows to the polished wood floor. Sarah peeked in and saw that the parlor opened into a small library with mahogany bookcases reaching as high as the twelve-foot ceiling. A cozy window seat adorned the alcove, full of plush red cushions and striped pillows. It looked like the perfect place to lose oneself in a book. The girls looked into the dining room to the right of the foyer; a circular staircase wound above them with the front desk of the inn nestled beneath it. So absorbed with her surroundings, it took Sarah a moment to notice a short, burly man standing behind the green marble counter wearing an oatmeal-colored sweater and chatting with another man on the other side of the counter.

Behind the front desk was a wide hallway and Sarah could just glimpse a large kitchen on the left. On the right side of the hallway was only one door and it was closed. The innkeeper looked up when he saw Sarah and the girls approaching. "Welcome to the Red Clover Inn." He sported a thatch of thick white hair, although he looked no older than forty-five.

The other man gave them a brief glance and headed for the stairs. "We'll talk later?"

"Sure," the innkeeper replied and turned his gaze back to Sarah and the girls. "You must be Mrs. Hart." He rounded the counter and reached out to shake her hand. "I'm Patrick Maguire. I believe we talked on the phone when you reserved your rooms."

"We did," Sarah affirmed, remembering her conversation. The man was rather chatty on the phone. "It's nice to meet you, Mr. Maguire."

A dimple flashed in his cheek. "I insist you call me Patrick." He turned to the twins. "And these must be your two lovely granddaughters."

"This is Audrey," Sarah said, placing one hand on Audrey's shoulder, "and her sister Amy."

Patrick's green eyes twinkled. "I hope you two are the adventurous type. I picked out a special room for you."

"What kind of room?" Audrey asked.

His smile widened. "You'll see." Then he turned back toward the front desk. "But first we need to get the three of you checked in. I was beginning to wonder if you were going to show up tonight."

"So was I." Sarah set her purse on the marble counter, the surface as smooth as glass. It was one of the few pieces of modern furniture in the room. "I tried to phone you, but my call wouldn't go through."

"Cell phone reception is pretty spotty around these parts. I've got a landline phone here," he said, nodding toward the cordless unit on his desk, "if you need to make a call."

"Actually, we do." She turned to the girls. "Why don't you call your folks and let them know we arrived?"

"Talk as long as you like," Patrick told them, reaching for the can of soda on the counter. He handed the receiver to Audrey and set the guest registry in front of Sarah.

"I want to call," Amy said, grabbing for the phone.

Audrey pulled it out of her grasp. "He gave it to me."

"Girls," Sarah said. "Just take turns. Audrey, you talk first and then give the phone to your sister."

She turned back to the counter. "Now, where would you like me to sign?"

"Right here," he said, his finger weaving over the registry before he planted it on a blank line below the name Dorothy Ogden. "My printer's out of ink or I'd print out a copy of your registration. I'll make sure you get a receipt before you check out."

"That's fine."

"Would you like a wake-up call for breakfast or do you want to sleep in?"

"We need to leave for Hartford by eight." She could hear Audrey telling her parents about their trip while Amy hovered over her, begging for her turn. "What time is breakfast?"

"Nine o'clock," Patrick said and took another swig of his soda. "But I always have coffee, juice, and rolls set out for the early birds."

"That sounds perfect." Sarah capped the pen. "I just hope the weather is decent."

"Should be sunny and clear. We're just catching the very edge of a storm front right now, but according to the latest weather report it's moving to the north."

Sarah breathed a sigh of relief. "That's good to hear."

A lanky young man emerged from the back carrying a yellow plastic sack.

"Where have you been?" Patrick said to him.

The young man swept the curtain of shaggy brown hair off his forehead and held up the sack in his hand. "I went to find salt for the front walk like you told me."

"That was almost half an hour ago," Patrick said and strained out a smile as he turned back to Sarah. "Would you take these ladies' suitcases up to their rooms?"

"Okay." He set the sack on the floor.

"Don't put it there," Patrick said. "If the salt leaks out it could ruin the floor. Put it back in the pantry first."

As the young man picked up the sack and headed for the kitchen, Sarah heard him muttering something unintelligible under his breath.

"This way, ladies." Patrick rounded the counter and escorted them to the stately mahogany staircase.

Sarah glanced around the main floor as they walked, impressed by the arched doorways, intricately carved woodwork, and lofty plank ceiling. "This is a beautiful building. I feel like I've stepped back into the past."

"Thank you," Patrick replied. "It takes a lot of work to maintain a place like this, but I think it's worth it."

Sarah agreed. Everything was pristine and well polished, including the brass chandeliers that lit their path up the staircase and dotted the hallway ceiling on the second floor.

When they reached the top of the stairs, they walked past several closed doors, their footsteps silent on the plush floral hall runner. Sarah was surprised they didn't encounter any other guests and then glanced at her watch and saw that it was almost eleven o'clock.

"Here we are, girls," Patrick announced as he opened the door in front of them. "This is your room for the weekend."

Amy and Audrey's eyes widened when they saw the huge bearskin rug in the center of the floor. The black bear's head was still attached and the mouth was open wide enough to reveal razor sharp teeth.

"Is that real?" Audrey gasped, pointing to the bearskin rug.

Patrick chuckled. "No, it's just a really good imitation. I found it in the attic when I bought the place and knew I had to use it in one of the guest rooms. I had a lot of fun decorating this one.

Sarah almost giggled at the awe-struck expressions on the girls' faces. She glanced around the rest of the room, taking in the rustic log furniture, forest green drapes, and king-size bed.

"This is pretty cool." Amy walked into the room and shrugged off her coat. Then she pulled her cell phone out of her pocket and began to take pictures of the room.

"I'm glad you like it," Patrick said and turned to Audrey. "How about you?"

"It's nice, I guess." Audrey looked down at the rug. "I'm just glad that wasn't a real bear."

"No dangerous animals here. And even if there were, your grandma's room is right through here."

Sarah followed him through the connecting door while the twins stayed behind to explore their room. After seeing that bearskin rug, Sarah was ready for anything. But when Patrick opened the door to her room, she was pleasantly surprised by the tranquil, Victorian atmosphere.

"How lovely." Sarah walked over to the rosewood sleigh bed. She ran one hand along the faded green, blue, and yellow patches of the antique quilt. "You don't see this Grandmother's Puzzle pattern very often."

"I thought it was fitting since you're traveling with your granddaughters." He pointed to a sepia portrait on the wall. "That's my grandmother, Maeve Ryan Maguire. She immigrated here from Ireland when she was twelve years old, but she never lost her Irish brogue nor her love for the old country."

"She must have been very special if you designed a room in her honor."

Patrick didn't reply, his eyelids drooping as if he were dozing off. Then he popped them open again, his gaze unfocused. He didn't smell like alcohol, but that could not have been plain old cola he was drinking.

"She was special," Patrick said after the awkward pause. "She helped raise me after my mum died and never put up with any nonsense."

Sarah could hear the love in his voice. She walked over to study the portrait. The woman's expression was very somber, like most photographic subjects of that era, but Sarah could see a sparkle in her eyes and the strong set of her shoulders. "What a wonderful portrait for you to remember her by."

"It is," Patrick agreed. "Most of the furniture in this room belonged to her, and she made those lace curtains. I wanted to put all of her things to good use, since she taught me how to make do with what I have."

A knock at the door made them both turn. "That must be Levi," Patrick said, walking over to open it.

The young man walked into the room carrying a suitcase in each hand and one tucked under his arm. "Where would you like me to set these, ma'am?"

"Just put them down anywhere," Sarah said as the girls walked through the connecting door into her room.

Levi set the suitcases by the bed, then glanced over at Patrick. "Anything else you want me to do before I clock out for the night?"

"Wait for me downstairs," Patrick told him.

Sarah reached into her purse and retrieved a couple of dollar bills for Levi. "Thank you for bringing up our bags."

"You're welcome." Levi took the money from her before turning and walking out the door, leaving it open behind him.

Patrick turned back to Sarah, his smile in place once more. "Now, as you can see, each room has a private bath and they're fully stocked with towels and toiletries. There are extra blankets in the closet and you'll find the television remote control in the drawer of your nightstand. We only have televisions in the guest rooms, there are none down-stairs."

"Do you have Internet?" Audrey asked him.

"Sorry," Patrick said, "we like to keep things simple around here."

"I think we can survive off-line for one weekend," Sarah said.

"Is there anything else you need?" he asked. "Of course, you're welcome to spend time in the parlor if you're not ready for bed yet."

"No, we're fine." Sarah told him. "We have a big day tomorrow—"

"Maguire," a voice said from the hallway.

Patrick turned around as the man who had been talking with him in the lobby appeared in the open doorway. "Yes?"

"Finish our conversation?" the man asked, then noticed Sarah. He tilted his head toward the hallway in a not-so-subtle manner. "In private?"

"Sure," Patrick said to him.

The man gave him a brisk nod. "I'll be downstairs."

Patrick moved to follow him. "See you in the morning, ladies."

"Good night." Sarah closed the door behind him, wondering if the man who was so rude was an employee or a guest. When she turned around she saw both girls frowning at her. "What's wrong?"

"We don't have to go to bed yet, do we?" Amy asked.

"It *is* pretty late," Sarah replied.

"But it's Friday night," Audrey said. "We always get to stay up later on the weekend. Please, Grandma."

"Please," echoed Amy.

Despite their long faces, Sarah had fought these bedtime battles with her own children and knew a tired child when she saw one. At the moment, there were two of them standing in front of her.

"As I told Mr. Maguire, we have a full day ahead of us tomorrow." She walked over to the girls and placed an arm around each one. "You two put on your pajamas and get in bed. You can read or watch television until you fall asleep."

Audrey looked like she wanted to argue, but Amy picked up her suitcase. "Let's just go to bed, Audrey. We don't have to fall asleep yet."

"Good night, girls," Sarah said as she watched them walk back to their room.

"Good night," they mumbled.

Sarah slipped off her wool coat and set her purse on the pink marble-topped dresser. She caught a glimpse of herself in the oval mirror, grimaced, and reached into her purse for a comb.

After she had tamed her graying blonde hair, she opened the top drawer of the dresser to place her comb inside and found an old Bible nestled there. She smoothed her fingers over the white leather cover, then carefully opened it.

After turning a few blank pages, she found the name Maeve Ryan inscribed in spidery black ink, along with a verse from Matthew 6:21: "For where your treasure is, there your heart will be also."

She turned the next page and found a family tree spanning both pages. Sarah carefully traced the branches, finding Maeve's name below the names of her parents and grandparents. She'd been born in 1920 and married a man named John Maguire in 1938. They'd had one child, Shawn Maguire, born in 1942. Shawn had married Mary Kerr and their son, Patrick Shawn Maguire, had been born in 1966.

But that wasn't the only bit of information she gleaned from Maeve's Bible. Patrick had married a woman named Hope Weaver in 1988, although Sarah hadn't seen a wedding ring on his left hand and there was no sign of family at the inn. There were no new branches added to the family tree after that, although someone had scribbled in Maeve's death in 1988. She assumed Patrick had written it, since he seemed so close to his grandmother.

She paged through the Bible, noting that Maeve had underlined several passages. It had obviously been well read and well loved. She placed the Bible back in the drawer and closed it, envying Patrick for owning such a precious treasure from his grandmother.

The house creaked and moaned under the force of the winter wind. She walked over to the window and pulled back the Irish lace curtain, only to find the window pane covered with a sheet of ice, distorting the shape of the trees outside. She shivered as frigid air slipped through tiny cracks in the old window. Sarah let the curtain fall from her hand and walked over to her suitcase to retrieve a cardigan. That's when she realized she had left her laptop computer in the car. She needed it to put the finishing touches on tomorrow's workshop presentation.

With a groan, Sarah donned her coat once more, walked over to the twins' room, and stuck her head inside. Amy lay in bed reading while Audrey sat on the bed next to her looking at pictures on her cell phone.

"I need to run down to the car for a minute, girls. I'll be right back."

"Okay," Amy said, not looking up from her book. "We'll be here."

"We're still wide awake," Audrey added, her words ending on a yawn.

Sarah smiled to herself as she walked downstairs, but her smile faded when she reached the front door. Wind rattled the brass doorknob, as if trying to gain entrance. The last thing she wanted to do was go out in that ice storm again.

She readied herself and opened the door to a flurry of tiny ice pellets. She stepped carefully out onto the front step, the pavement slick under her feet. She grasped the handrail, also covered with ice, and made her way gingerly down the steps.

The treacherous walk to her car seemed to take ages, the wind constantly trying to push her back. She leaned forward, head down, the inky darkness and driving sleet making it difficult to see more than a few feet in front of her.

When she finally reached the car, she inserted the key into the trunk and struggled to open it. Ice had filled the crevices, making it necessary for her to yank on the trunk lid several times before the icy bond finally broke.

She reached inside the trunk and pulled out her laptop case, eager to return to the inn. The wind was at her back now, making her journey back to the inn a little less arduous.

Sarah savored the warmth as she walked through the front door, her body shivering. Then she heard something odd. She paused, her ears perked, before she realized the noise was the sound of a scuffle coming from the parlor.

She walked over in time to see a man hurrying out of the room. He had his back to her, so she couldn't see his face. He favored his right leg as he walked and soon disappeared into the shadows.

She turned toward the parlor and saw Patrick standing with one hand braced against the fireplace mantle.

"Patrick, are you okay?" she asked.

"Oh I'm fine. Just a slight...disagreement." Patrick rubbed one hand over his eyes. "It's the plight of an innkeeper to deal with demanding guests."

She sensed he was glossing over the incident and could see him struggling to retain both his balance and his composure. "Are you sure you're all right? Can I get you anything?"

"No, no, I'm fine," he said with a dismissive wave. "I usually try to be as accommodating as possible, but some people just can't be satisfied. I'm sorry if we disturbed you."

"Not at all," she assured him, still uneasy about what she'd just witnessed. "I just had to get my laptop out of my car."

He nodded, but didn't seem to be listening. He closed his eyes and leaned his head back against the stone chimney.

"Well, good night again," she said, heading toward the stairs.

"Good night."

Sarah returned to her room and checked on the girls, who were both fast asleep. She tucked the bed's vintage quilt around their shoulders, kissed each girl on the forehead, and returned to her own room.

For the next hour, she struggled to stay awake while she worked on the laptop. She even nodded off once, until the sound of a door slamming somewhere below woke her up again.

When she finally climbed into bed, she welcomed the heavy quilt and coverlet, still feeling slightly chilled from her trip to the car. Her eyes drifted shut as soon as her head hit the pillow and she fell into a dreamless sleep.

The muffled sounds of a baby crying awakened her in the middle of the night. She turned over and glanced at the clock on the antique nightstand.

Three o'clock.

She groaned, turned over, and closed her eyes again. Sleet continued to batter the windowpane and the howling wind competed with the baby's cries. She'd always had trouble sleeping in a strange bed, and the creaks and groans of the unfamiliar house made it difficult for her to fall back to sleep.

Thirty minutes later, the wind calmed and the baby finally stopped crying. Sarah closed her eyes again, knowing she had precious few hours of slumber left. After several moments of blessed silence, she finally drifted off into a deep sleep.

The next thing she knew, a bloodcurdling scream ripped through the air.

 **CHAPTER TWO**

S arah sat up in bed, her heart thudding heavily inside her chest. The scream sounded like it had come from a woman and she sounded terrified.

Sarah's feet hit the floor just as the connecting door to the twins' room came flying open and banged against the wall. Light shone through the window as Audrey and Amy rushed to her bed, their bare feet slapping against the wood floor.

"Grandma, what was that?" Audrey exclaimed, fear in her eyes.

"I don't know." Sarah hastily dug her feet into the slippers her best friend Martha had crocheted for her and grabbed her flannel robe. "You two wait here while I go see what's happened. Lock the door behind me."

Amy clutched her arm. "No, Grandma, we want to go with you."

Audrey nodded. "Please don't make us stay here alone."

Sarah hesitated only a moment. "All right, you can come with me."

The girls followed Sarah out of the room as they heard another scream, followed by a plaintive cry. "Please, someone help me!"

The woman's voice was coming from downstairs.

Sarah hurried down the hallway, the girls on her heels, as other guest room doors began to open. A chubby, middle-aged man stepped out of his room, followed by a petite woman with a mop of salt-and-pepper hair. They wore matching green warm-up suits and white tennis shoes.

"What's going on?" the woman asked as Sarah hurried by them.

"I don't know," Sarah replied.

Muffled sobs came from below. Others followed as Sarah and the twins rushed down the stairs and into the parlor. An elderly woman stood alone next to an overturned love seat, her thin face ashen. She was dressed in a black pinstripe suit and a pair of sensible black shoes.

"Are you all right?" Sarah asked, sidestepping an upended coffee table as she rushed over to the woman. The parlor looked as if it had been ransacked. Tables and chairs had been overturned, along with a potted ficus tree, the rich black potting soil spilling over the wood floor.

"Look," the woman cried, pointing a shaky finger at the Persian rug in front of her.

Sarah looked and saw blood. A lot of blood. It had pooled on the center of the rug and thinned out into a long, red streak that ran to the edge of the floral pattern.

"What happened?" Sarah asked.

"I don't know," the woman breathed, wobbling a little. "I came down here and saw...." Her words trailed off as her knees buckled.

Sarah caught her beneath the arms just before she hit the floor. The man Sarah had seen the night before rushed over and helped steady the woman. They half-carried her to one of the few chairs still standing in the parlor.

"Just sit still for a moment," Sarah advised as she knelt down in front of the woman. "Put your head between your knees and take some slow, deep breaths."

Sarah followed her own advice and took a few deep breaths herself. She glanced at the twins, who were both wide-eyed and pale but looked more curious than frightened now. Then she surveyed the rest of the people in the room.

The man who had been talking with Patrick Maguire at the front desk wore the same gray suit she'd seen him in last night, only this time he'd added a black eye to go with his outfit. The green warm-up suit couple stood holding on to each other, both groomed and dressed, as if they'd been up for a while.

There was also a young girl, not more than twenty, who held a baby in her arms. Most likely the same baby who had cried for so long last night, now sleeping peacefully in the pink wool blanket her mother had wrapped around her.

"Where is Mr. Maguire?" Sarah said aloud, suddenly realizing the innkeeper was nowhere in sight.

"I don't know." The man in the gray suit looked around the room. "Maybe he didn't hear all the commotion."

"I'll go check his room," the green warm-up suit woman said. "Maybe he knows what happened here."

"I'm coming with you, Vonnie," her husband said, following her out of the room. "I don't want you going anywhere alone."

Sarah watched them leave and turned back to the shaken woman in the chair. "I'm Sarah. Are you okay?"

The older woman slowly nodded. "I'm...Dorothy."

"Can you tell us what happened, Dorothy?"

Dorothy closed her eyes as she recounted the incident. "I came downstairs to make myself a cup of herbal tea—for my arthritis. Patrick told me I was welcome to use the kitchen any time I wanted. But when I saw all the lights on in the parlor, I thought something must be going on. Then I noticed the blood on the rug...." She shuddered and opened her green eyes. "I just started screaming and couldn't stop. I don't know what came over me."

Sarah reached out to pat her hand, finding it cold and clammy. "I'm sure it was a shock for you. Did you hear anything on your way down? Or any other time last night?"

Dorothy shook her head and pointed to her ears. "Earplugs."

Sarah turned around. "Did anyone else hear or see anything last night?"

"Just the wind howling all night," the man in the gray suit said, "and that baby crying."

The young mother shielded her baby's face from the blood-soaked parlor, her blue eyes wide as she looked around the room. "Why is there so much blood?"

Before anyone could reply, the warm-up suit woman and her husband returned. "Mr. Maguire isn't in his room. He's not in the kitchen either."

"Are you sure?" the man in the gray suit asked.

She nodded. "Chuck pounded on his bedroom door and called out to him," the woman replied. "The door was locked, so I can't say for certain, but there's no way Mr. Maguire couldn't have heard him."

The sound of a door closing toward the back of the inn made them all turn toward the kitchen. A moment later, a man appeared in the doorway wearing a parka, the long hood concealing his face.

"Mr. Maguire?" Sarah asked hopefully and realized her mistake when the man pushed the hood back. "Oh, it's you."

Levi looked around the parlor and at the guests gathered there. His face was red, chapped from the cold wind. "What's going on?"

"We don't know," Sarah told him. "Dorothy here found the parlor like this when she came downstairs this morning.

We can't find Mr. Maguire and there's blood...." She pointed out the rug stain to him.

Levi moved closer to her, his gaze fixed on the blood-stained rug. "Patrick is missing?"

The man in the gray suit sighed. "I don't suppose you have security cameras installed in this place, do you?"

"Of course not," Levi replied. "There's never been any need."

"I think we should call the police," Sarah said. "It's obvious someone's been seriously hurt, possibly Mr. Maguire—Patrick—himself."

"The police can't help us," Levi said.

The elderly woman named Dorothy looked up at him, her forehead crinkled. "Why not?"

Levi walked over to the window and parted the gold velvet drapes. "That's why."

A flurry of white greeted them. The blowing snow was so thick Sarah could barely make out her car in the parking lot. Amy and Audrey ran to the window.

"Wow," Amy exclaimed, "I've never seen so much snow before."

Sarah had never seen so much *blood* before. Someone had been seriously hurt. Quite possibly by one of the guests gathered in the parlor.

Levi pulled off his gloves and stuffed them in the pockets of his coat. "It was snowing when I left Hartford this morning and by the time I hit the gravel drive it was blinding. The radio traffic report listed so many accidents, they finally stopped trying to keep up with them all."

"You're lucky you made it here," the man in the warm-up suit said.

"I almost didn't," Levi said. "My car got stuck about a half mile from the inn so I walked through the snow to get here. Now I can't feel my fingers or toes."

The warm-up suit woman walked over to him and pulled him toward the fireplace. "Come sit by the fire and take your shoes off." She helped him pull off his leather work boots revealing a pair of red wool socks. "It's going to hurt a little when you start warming up, but it's better than losing some toes to frostbite."

Sarah watched her tend to Levi, thankful he'd found his way through the blizzard. What if the snowstorm had started last night when she and the girls were lost on the country roads? She swallowed hard at that disturbing thought, aware of how quickly the New England weather could change in February.

But another storm was brewing inside the inn—one that felt just as dangerous as the blizzard outside. "We need to call the police," Sarah said, "and report what happened here."

The man in the gray suit turned to her. "You heard the kid. The roads are impassable. The police won't make it out here now. They wouldn't even if they didn't have so many accidents out there to deal with."

"But they'll be here eventually." Sarah walked over to the front counter to use the landline. "They can tell us what to do until then."

"That's right," Dorothy said, a little more color in her cheeks now. "We have to do something."

Sarah picked up the cordless receiver, but there was no dial tone. After checking the cord connection, she placed it back on the base. "The phone is dead."

Levi winced as he shifted his feet next to the hearth. "The phone lines always go down in bad weather. We're lucky we still have electricity."

"So what are we supposed to do now?" the young mother said. "We can't leave and we can't call for help. We don't know who's been hurt and if one of us might be next!"

Sarah pulled her robe more tightly around her as she tried to calm her own fears. "Let's not panic."

"But he said we could lose electricity," the young woman said, pointing at Levi. Her voice grew more strained. "How am I supposed to warm up my baby's bottle without electricity?"

"We'll survive just fine without electricity if it comes to that," Sarah said, hoping it was true. "People did it for thousands of years. We can a build a fire, after all."

"That's right," Levi said. "We have a backup generator too. But if worse comes to worst, there's plenty of kindling out in the shed. Heat won't be a problem and we'll have lots of natural light during the day."

The young woman didn't look convinced. "But what if someone gets sick? What if we have an emergency and we can't get to a hospital?"

"In case you haven't noticed, we already have an emergency," the man in the gray suit said. "Somebody decided to use this rug as a bandage. Too bad he didn't leave a trail or we could find out where he went."

That's right, Sarah realized. Why wasn't there a trail of blood to follow?

She studied the rug again, the dark stain of blood easy to discern on the pale carpet fibers. Why did the blood trail suddenly stop at the edge of the rug? From the amount of blood on the carpet, whoever had been wounded must have bled for a while. Obviously, someone didn't want to leave a trail—either the injured party or, more likely, the person who had caused the injury.

"We need to find Patrick," Sarah announced. "Levi, do you know if there's a key to his room anywhere?"

"Yeah." Levi tested his stocking feet on the floor and slowly stood up. "There are spare keys to all the rooms in the desk."

"I'm not sure you should be walking anywhere yet," the warm-up suit woman warned him.

Levi took a few faltering steps toward the registration desk and then picked up the pace. "My feet feel a lot better now."

"Just keep an eye on your toes," she called after him. "If they start to turn purple, that's a bad sign."

After Levi retrieved the key, they all started to follow him out of the room. Sarah glanced back to see the young mother hesitating, her baby starting to fuss in her arms.

"Are you coming—I'm sorry, I don't know your name."

"Natalie," the girl said softly. "I'm Natalie and this is Bella."

Sarah walked over to her, placing a hand on her shoulder. "I'm Sarah. I think we should stay together, Natalie. We'll all be safer that way."

The girl gave a slow nod and walked out of the parlor with the others.

"Patrick!" Levi shouted as they walked past the desk and down the wide hallway on the way to the innkeeper's room. "Patrick, where are you?"

"Maguire?" the man in the warm-up suit—Chuck, his wife Vonnie had called him—shouted, cupping his hands around his mouth. "Get out here!"

The shouts echoed through the house, but there was no response.

When they finally reached Patrick's room near the end of the hallway, an eerie silence settled among them. His room was located on the right side of the house. Levi inserted the key into the lock and slowly opened the door.

"Patrick?" Levi called out as he stepped over the threshold. "You in here?"

Sarah and the other guests followed him into Patrick's room. It was a large suite with a king-size bed at one end and a sitting room with a black leather sofa and a matching recliner at the other.

Levi walked over to the bathroom where the door stood open. He stuck his head inside and then backed out again. "He's not in there."

"Do you see any blood?" Sarah asked, noting that the bedroom was pristine. It looked as if Patrick's bed hadn't even been slept in. A vintage shamrock quilt lay smooth and neat atop the white flannel sheets.

"No, nothing." Levi scratched his ear. "It's weird, isn't it?"

"Very," Sarah said, walking over to his dresser. "His keys and wallet are here."

Vonnie, the woman in the warm-up suit, sighed. "So that means Patrick has to be here. He couldn't walk anywhere in this weather."

He might not be able to walk at all, Sarah thought to herself as she picked up the brown leather wallet and opened it. She saw Patrick's driver's license through a clear plastic pocket, as well as a stack of credit cards in their respective slots and three twenty-dollar bills neatly lined up in the fold.

Levi moved toward the dresser to examine the key ring. "That's the key to his truck," he said, pointing out the large silver key. "And this gold one is the key to the front and back doors of the inn."

Dorothy stepped forward. "Was the door locked when you arrived this morning?"

Levi nodded. "The backdoor was locked. I had to use my key to get in. I haven't checked the front."

"Does anyone else have a key to this place, other than you and Patrick?" Sarah asked.

"Nope."

"Well, Vonnie was right," Chuck said. "Even if Patrick did go out the front door, he wouldn't have gotten far without a car."

Sarah set the wallet back on the dresser. There was nothing else there. Nothing that could tell her anything about Patrick or what might have happened to him.

She needed to dig deeper.

Sarah decided to check the bathroom out herself. It looked as pristine as the bedroom. Two white terry cloth towels were neatly hung on the rack and the porcelain sink and shower shone to a high polish. It was almost too clean. She sniffed, detecting a faint hint of bleach in the air.

When she walked out of the bathroom everyone stood around the room casting uneasy glances at each other. They were all strangers to Sarah and to each other. That would have to change if they wanted to find Patrick.

"It's Patrick's blood in the parlor, isn't it," Dorothy said, her arms wrapped around her thin waist. "Something awful happened to him, didn't it?"

"It looks that way," Sarah said softly.

"Then that means...." Vonnie's voice trailed off as she moved closer to her husband.

"Someone here hurt him," her husband said bluntly.

"And we're trapped here," Natalie whispered, her eyes wide with fear. "We can't leave."

"And neither can the person who attacked Patrick." Levi looked at each one of them.

Sarah took a deep breath, wishing she could dismiss that possibility, but it was all too real. "I think we all need to stick together until this mystery is solved," Sarah said and turned to the twins. "I don't want you girls going anywhere without me. Understood? The three of us stick together at all times."

They both gave a solemn nod. Then Amy said, "Grandma, does this mean we're all in danger?"

CHAPTER THREE

T hat's exactly what it means," the man in the gray suit said. "It's possible any one of us could be next."

No one said anything as his words sank in. Audrey nestled closer to Sarah, while Amy fixed her gaze on the man. After a moment or two, Bella emitted a halfhearted cry, breaking the silence.

Natalie gently patted the baby's back until she settled quietly against her shoulder once more. "What are we going to do?"

"I think we should search the house," Sarah replied, refusing to let fear stop her from looking for Patrick. She couldn't stay locked in her room when a man might lie bleeding to death somewhere near.

"Do you think that's safe?" Chuck asked.

"Safe or not, we need to gather first-aid supplies," Vonnie said. "To help Patrick and ourselves, if it comes to that."

"Besides, his attacker is probably right here in this room," the man in the gray suit said dryly. "We're all as safe as we're going to get until the roads are cleared."

His words descended on the room like a dark cloud. Sarah wrapped her arms around the twins, pulling them closer to her. The other guests looked at each other warily.

"As long as we stick together," Sarah said, trying to keep her voice steady, "we should be all right. Patrick needs our help. We have to find him as soon as possible."

"She's right," Vonnie agreed. "I've been a nursing assistant for over twenty years, so I know first aid and basic medical care. We need to find him as quickly as possible.

"Then let's start the search," Dorothy said. "That's the only way we'll discover what really happened in that parlor."

"And who's to blame," Chuck added. "I'm sorry, I didn't catch your name," he said to the man in the gray suit.

"Finn Hawkins," the man said. Sarah's gaze landed on Hawkins's black eye. Had he been the one scuffling with Patrick in the parlor last night? She hadn't seen enough of the man to identify him. It could be any of the men in this room—Chuck, or Levi for that matter, but Finn Hawkins was the one sporting the shiner.

He saw her looking at him. "Well, what are we waiting for? Why don't you ladies search upstairs and we'll search the main floor."

"We're all sticking together," Natalie told him. "Remember?"

He rolled his eyes. "This search will go a lot faster if we break up into groups."

Levi ran his hand through his brown hair, still slightly damp from the heavy snow falling outside. "No, she's right. We don't know who or what we might find. Even if no one broke in, Patrick might have let someone in."

Sarah stepped forward, not wanting to waste another moment. "Levi, why don't you lead the way since you know this place best. We can start with the second floor."

Levi gave a brisk nod, turned, and headed for the front desk. He retrieved the set of spare keys, everyone following him toward the circular staircase.

Amy held tight to Sarah's elbow and whispered. "Hey, Grandma?"

"Yes, dear?"

"Are you scared?"

Sarah reached for her hand and gave it a squeeze. "A little bit. Are you?"

"Yeah," Amy whispered.

"Me too," Audrey said.

"Everything will be okay. I won't let anything happen to you," Sarah promised, and prayed silently asking God to help her keep that promise.

When the group passed by the front entrance, they stopped to check the door.

Chuck turned the dead bolt and tried to pull open the door, but it wouldn't budge. "It was locked. And it's frozen shut."

Finn moved beside him and pounded his fist along the door frame, trying to loosen the ice frozen there. Levi joined them and in a few minutes they were able to pull the door open. Snow flew in on a blast of wind, swirling flakes around them and spilling the snow piled on the porch onto the rug.

Levi steadied himself against the door frame as he peered outside. "I don't see any footprints out here or anything unusual."

"Then let's shut the door before we all freeze to death," Finn said, brushing snow off his sleeves.

Levi closed the door, bolted it, and continued on to the staircase.

As they climbed the stairs, Audrey whispered, "Is everybody going to look at our room too?"

"I suppose so," Sarah replied, "since we're searching the entire house. Why?"

"It's kind of a mess." Audrey looked at Amy. "You left your clothes all over the floor."

"I was going to pick them up this morning," Amy retorted. "I just didn't have time."

"You should have just put the clothes back in your suitcase last night," Audrey said.

"Gross. I can't put dirty clothes back in my suitcase with the clean ones."

"I don't think anyone is going to care what your room looks like," Sarah said. "The important thing is to find Patrick and help him."

Amy looked up at her. "So you think it really is his blood on the rug?"

Sarah nodded. "He seemed so proud of this place. I can't imagine he would just abandon it willingly without telling anyone—especially in this awful weather."

"I hope he's okay," Audrey said as they reached the top of the stairs.

Levi turned to the group. "How do you want to handle this?"

No one said anything for a moment and then Sarah pointed to the first door. "Let's just start here and work our way down the hall."

"This is the Thayers' room," Levi began, sorting through the keys in his hands.

"I'll do it," Vonnie said, stepping in front of him to unlock the door. "Hope you all don't mind a little clutter."

Sarah walked through the open doorway. Clutter was an understatement. She stared at the disaster inside, wondering how Chuck and Vonnie were able to move through the debris of papers and clothes littering the bed and floor.

She could barely make out the pattern of the Island Path quilt on the rattan bed and almost tripped over a wicker stool hidden beneath a pile of clothes. A bamboo ceiling fan adorned the ceiling and a pair of white athletic socks hung from a large tiki mask by the bed.

"Do you suppose Patrick's buried under here somewhere?" Levi joked, gingerly nudging a pile of damp towels with his foot.

"He's not in here." Vonnie crossed her arms over her chest. She was as thin as her husband was plump, with a mop of curls on top of her head and hazel eyes. "You can search if you like."

"I think I will," Finn said, stepping into the chaos, "if you don't mind."

Chuck shrugged his shoulders. "Be our guest."

Finn found a path to the bed and looked underneath it as the rest of the group observed near the doorway, unable to come farther into the room without stepping on the Thayers' belongings.

Chuck walked over to his wife and whispered something. Her mouth thinned and she shook her head. Chuck glanced over at Levi and whispered something to his wife again.

Sarah tried to find another path among the debris to edge closer to the couple so she could hear what they were saying.

"I told you this would happen," Sarah heard Chuck whisper to his wife.

"Now isn't the time to panic," Vonnie muttered back.

"We have to—," he began, and then he saw Sarah coming and closed his mouth.

"Do you need something?" Vonnie asked her.

"I just want to check out the bathroom," Sarah hedged, circling around them. She poked her head inside the cluttered bathroom, but didn't see anything suspicious.

Finn opened the closet wide enough for everyone to see inside. Sarah noticed it was the cleanest spot in the room since most of the Thayers' clothes littered the floor.

"No Patrick," Finn announced, closing the closet door.

"I knew that," Vonnie said, tipping up her chin.

An uneasy tension filled the hallway as the group continued toward the next guest room.

"This is my room," Dorothy said, unlocking the door for them and leading the way inside.

Unlike the Thayers' room, Dorothy's bedroom could have passed a white-glove test. The bed was neatly made with an Evening Star quilt. The white pillows were fluffed, and a pale yellow blanket embroidered with blue violets was draped over the trellis-style quilt rack in the corner.

Levi looked under the bed and Finn shook his head. "Does this seem silly to anyone else? I mean, do we really think Patrick is hiding under a bed?"

"If you don't have anything to hide, why would you care?" Natalie asked him, shifting the still sleeping Bella to the other shoulder.

Finn threw his hands up. "Carry on."

Sarah didn't see any blood stains near the bed or any signs of a struggle in the room. A quick check of the closet and bathroom revealed nothing new. She was about to follow the rest of the guests out the door when she saw something that looked like a spot of blood near the vintage seed catalog displayed atop the dresser.

She walked over to examine it and realized it was a dried rose petal, probably from the potpourri in the bowl next to the catalog. With a sigh of disappointment, she dropped the petal back into the bowl and joined the others making their way back into the hallway.

They searched the twins' room next and the group moved on to Sarah's room; neither revealed any surprises or hidden bodies.

When they reached Natalie's room, the young woman carefully dug into the pocket of her pink pajama pants to avoid disturbing the baby and handed the key to Audrey. "Will you unlock it for me?"

"Sure." Audrey opened the door and stepped aside so the rest of the guests could enter.

The entire room had a light, airy feel to it, thanks to the fluffy white clouds and blue sky painted on the ceiling. Sarah rounded a bag of disposable diapers as she looked over the room. A pile of burp cloths sat on the dresser next to a pair of baby bottles and a ceramic dove figurine.

Natalie fussed about the room, straightening the Flying Geese quilt on her bed and picking up a stuffed teddy bear that lay near the decorative birdcage in the corner. Then Natalie's gaze moved to the travel crib near her bed. "I wish I could lay Bella down, but I shouldn't leave her alone, should I?"

"I think she's safer with you," Sarah said. She looked at Audrey who had been following Natalie around admiring Bella all morning. "We'll help you if she wakes up, won't we, Audrey?"

"We sure will."

"I can help too, Grandma," Amy said.

Before she could reply, Finn spoke. "Let's just get one thing clear before we get to my room. All my papers and personal belongings are off-limits, so keep your hands to yourselves."

Levi arched a brow. "Is there something you're trying to hide?"

"Not at all," Finn replied. "But there are confidential work documents in my room and it's obvious that at least one person among us can't be trusted."

Dorothy leaned toward Sarah and whispered. "If you ask me, Finn's the one we can't trust. That black eye didn't come from slipping out of bed this morning."

Sarah nodded, still trying to wrap her mind around the fact that one of these people could have caused that bloody mess in the parlor. And, even worse, had taken Patrick somewhere when he obviously needed medical attention— unless it had been too late. Sarah prayed they'd find Patrick in time to help.

Finn led the way to his room and opened the door. "Let's make this quick. I'm getting hungry."

Sarah didn't know how he could think about food at a time like this. A tense knot had formed in her stomach and she knew it wouldn't unravel until Patrick was found.

She stepped inside Finn's room, her gaze scanning the papers laid out across the Railroad Crossing quilt on his antique iron bed. Just like Levi, Sarah wondered what Finn had to hide.

"Did the toy train come with the room?" Chuck asked, checking out the elaborate model train set on the long table in the corner. The track formed a figure eight and the set included a train station, miniature people, and plastic trees and cows.

"Yeah, this room is perfect for a nine-year-old," Finn answered, never taking his eyes off Levi as the young man looked under the bed and checked the bathroom and closet.

"Or someone who acts like a nine-year-old," Natalie whispered to Audrey, who giggled.

The last guest room was empty, the air heavy with a musty scent that indicated it hadn't been used for days.

"We've been fighting a shower leak in this room," Levi said, standing near the open door, "so it's been out of commission for a while."

Sarah walked inside the room, her gaze drawn to the vintage Log Cabin quilt on the bed and moving to the gingham curtains at the window and the corncob pipe set on the dresser.

She thought an empty room was the perfect place to hide Patrick, but another thorough search left her feeling disappointed. The weariness of a sleepless night crept into her bones as they left the room and headed toward the attic.

"That room was even worse than mine," Finn murmured to Sarah. "It was like a Hee-Haw nightmare."

Sarah couldn't help but smile. She had liked the room, but she wasn't surprised that Finn Hawkins didn't. His personality screamed "big city," making it all the more curious that he'd chosen to stay at a remote country inn.

When they reached the attic stairs, Natalie moved aside. "I really don't want to take Bella up there. It will be cold and dusty."

"I'll stay here with you," Dorothy offered, "until they come back."

The rest of them climbed the narrow attic stairs single file, with Levi leading the way and Finn bringing up the rear. As they neared the top of the house, the wind grew louder and the air grew colder. The attic was dim and dusty, with cobwebs hanging from the exposed rafters and the smell of mildew in the air. A loud bang sounded in the stone chimney.

Vonnie screamed and jumped, bumping into Sarah. "What was that?"

"The wind, probably," Sarah said, her own heart pounding in her chest. "My chimney at home makes the same kind of noise when it's windy outside."

The woman visibly trembled, inducing her husband to reach out and steady her. "Are you all right?"

Vonnie took a deep breath and nodded. "I guess I'm just a little spooked after what happened this morning."

"Everybody okay back there?" Levi called out, still standing at the head of the group.

"We're fine," Sarah called back.

A series of narrow aisles had been left between all the boxes stacked on the attic floor, making Sarah feel like she was caught in a maze. She glimpsed boxes of newspapers and other documents that dated back decades. There was even an old Smith-Corona manual typewriter sitting on top of an antique bureau.

"Patrick?" Levi called out as he walked the length of the attic, the others close behind. "Patrick?"

Chuck and Finn tossed aside a pile of old lumpy mattresses stacked in one corner to see if there was anything beneath them, but all they found was a broken rocking chair. Other pieces of furniture were scattered about the attic, but nothing looked as if it had been disturbed. There was no sign of life. No clues that might lead them to Patrick.

Another bang sounded in the chimney and this time Sarah jumped. Audrey and Amy walked directly behind her as they all made their way back to the attic door and headed down the rickety steps. Dorothy and Natalie waited for them at the bottom of the stairs.

"This is probably as good a time as any for everyone to get dressed," Sarah said to the rest of the group. "We can meet in the hallway when we're ready to go back downstairs."

"Good idea," Natalie said, heading for her room.

Levi leaned against the wall. "Anyone who wants to search outside better grab your coat, gloves, and hat while we're up here," he advised. "It's too cold to go out in this weather without them."

Sarah and the girls hurried into their rooms, as did the other guests. "You two get dressed and brush your teeth," Sarah told them.

"Can we go outside with everybody?" Amy asked.

"Yes," Sarah replied, slipping out of her robe. "We're all sticking together for as long as it takes."

A short while later, the three of them joined the other guests in the hallway. Sarah felt more at ease now that she was wearing her powder blue pullover sweater and gray wool slacks instead of her flannel nightgown and robe.

The girls had each changed out of the sweatpants and T-shirt combo they'd worn to bed into another sweatpants and T-shirt combo. Sarah didn't understand why one pair was considered pajamas and the other was daywear, but she supposed it didn't matter as long as they were comfortable.

They all continued downstairs and headed for the kitchen, calling out for Patrick once more.

When they entered the kitchen, Sarah's gaze went to the clock on the stove. It was almost nine, which meant Patrick had been missing for at least three hours. If they didn't find him soon…She closed her eyes and whispered a prayer. "Lord, please protect my girls and all the people in this house. And watch over Patrick, Lord, wherever he may be."

"What's that?" Amy asked.

Sarah opened her eyes and saw her granddaughter pointing out the kitchen window. She saw a small building connected to the house by a covered portico. "It looks like a garage."

"It's more like a shed," Levi replied. "We keep the lawn mower and tools and stuff in it."

Chuck donned his coat as he headed for the screened porch at the back of the kitchen. "Let's get this over with."

Sarah made sure the twins were fully protected from head to toe before wrapping up in her own winter gear and heading for the backdoor. Dorothy once again remained behind with Natalie and the baby.

The covered portico protected them from the worst of the snow, but it still swirled around them, the cold stinging Sarah's throat as she breathed in. The twins walked just ahead of her, making a path in the snow.

It took only a few minutes for all of them to reach the shed, but Sarah's fingers were already tingling with cold by the time she walked through the shed door.

"It's not much warmer in here than it is outside," Vonnie exclaimed, her cheeks a bright red.

Finn looked around the small shed. "If Patrick's out here, he's probably frozen by now."

But it was easy to see that Patrick wasn't there. There was no blood on the oil-stained floor and the workbench held only tools.

Then Sarah noticed something under the workbench. She moved closer and saw several cans of gasoline tucked far under the counter. She could even smell the fumes now that she was close enough. Sarah knelt down and gave each a little shake to see if they were full. Why would Patrick need ten full cans of gasoline? The box of rags sitting right next to the cans looked a little suspect too. They also made her uneasy. She shoved the box away from the cans.

"Find something?" Finn asked, standing behind her.

She turned around and rose to her feet. "Ten cans of gasoline."

"Enough to make a pretty good bonfire," Finn said.

Sarah brushed the dust from her hands. "Let's hope it doesn't come to that."

Finn shivered, rubbing his gloved hands together. "Do you suppose if we stayed out here in the freezing cold long enough the guilty party would finally crack and confess?"

Before she could reply, glass shattered behind her. She turned around and saw Chuck leaning with his elbows on the workbench, head in his hands.

"I can't take this anymore," he cried. "What if he's buried in the snow somewhere?" He raked a hand through his thinning gray hair. "The wind and snow and cold just don't stop! They're driving me crazy!"

The twins hurried over to Sarah as Chuck shoved another empty bottle from the workbench onto the floor, the glass exploding against the concrete.

Vonnie moved toward him. "Let me fix you breakfast. I know that will make you feel better."

They all stared at the Thayers as Vonnie spoke softly to her husband. Chuck's shoulders slumped as he slowly nodded and they headed out the door.

"On second thought," Finn whispered to Sarah. "Maybe it's safer out here."

Despite his words, Sarah knew they had no choice but to follow Chuck and Vonnie back to the inn. She glanced over at the twins, both of them standing still with shock at Chuck's outburst. Sarah was shocked too, caught unprepared by Chuck's sudden display of temper.

When they reached the kitchen, Vonnie settled Chuck into a chair and poured him a glass of orange juice. He remained silent as he sipped the juice, his gaze on the floor.

"So what's for breakfast?" Finn asked, his question easing the tension in the room.

Levi held up his hands. "Don't look at me. Patrick always makes breakfast. I can't even boil water."

"I'll make it," Vonnie offered, walking over to the refrigerator and peering inside. "Looks like we've got bacon and eggs. Orange juice too. Will someone check the pantry for rolls?"

"I'll do it," Sarah moved to the back of the kitchen.

The walk-in pantry was much bigger than her pantry back home. The spicy aromas of cinnamon and sage tickled her nostrils. Strings of dried chili peppers hung from the ceiling, and home-canned vegetables and fruits lined the oak shelves on both sides of the pantry.

She took note of a yellow bag of potato chips and cans of tuna at the back of one shelf, keeping them in mind for lunch. The less time it took to prepare food, the more time they'd have to search for Patrick.

Then her gaze fell on the wide, gray steel door at the end of the pantry. It looked new and oddly out of place, the thick steel hinges gleaming in the light.

Oddest of all was the heavy padlock and chain keeping the door securely locked.

CHAPTER FOUR

I think you'd all better take a look at this." Sarah called out.

She waited until the others joined her in the pantry. It was a long, narrow room, about six feet deep, providing just enough space for them all to fit inside.

"I found this locked door." She cupped the padlock in her hand, noting the brand name, Sentinel, engraved across the front of it.

Finn turned to Levi. "Where does this door lead?"

"To the cellar," Levi replied, looking a little flustered. "I forgot all about it."

Sarah watched Chuck walk over and tug on the heavy padlock. Everyone tensed.

Chuck turned and Sarah heard someone suck in his breath. "Why is the door locked?" Chuck's voice was much calmer than it had been in the shed. "Got something valuable down there?"

"No, it's because the insurance guy told Patrick to lock it." Levi brushed his hair out of his eyes. "The stairs to the cellar can be dangerous."

"So he didn't want any guests wandering down there and possibly getting hurt?" Sarah said. She remembered Dorothy telling her that Patrick didn't mind if she used the kitchen to make herself a cup of tea. Maybe he'd had problems with guests snooping around the place when it was unattended.

"That's right," Levi said. "He didn't want anybody to sue him if they fell down the stairs."

"So where's the key?" Finn asked, testing the door with his hand. It didn't budge.

Levi pulled the key ring from his pocket and flipped through the keys. "It's supposed to be here, but I don't see it." He backed out of the pantry. "I'll check the front desk."

Vonnie looked around the pantry while they waited for Levi to return. "Does anyone see any canned spinach? That's got a lot of Vitamin K in it. Great for helping blood to clot. For when we find Patrick."

Sarah knew spinach wouldn't do Patrick much good if his bleeding hadn't stopped by now. Still, it didn't hurt to be prepared. She noticed an unopened package of white cotton dishcloths on the shelf above her.

"Could we use these for bandages?" Sarah asked, reaching for the package.

"Perfect." Vonnie said, taking them from her. "And I've got some anti-inflammatory pills for pain."

"I've got plenty of those too," Dorothy said. "For my arthritis."

"I suppose he might need stitches too," Vonnie added, "but that's beyond my scope of experience."

In truth, they wouldn't be able to do much if Patrick was seriously injured. Not as long as the blizzard kept them trapped here, far away from the nearest doctor or hospital.

A chill swept through Sarah. Even if they found him alive, it might not matter. *Please, Lord, don't let us be too late.*

Levi returned to the pantry. "The key is gone."

Dorothy frowned. "Are you sure? Maybe it was just misplaced."

Levi shrugged. "All I know is that it's not anywhere it's supposed to be."

"Great," Finn rubbed his temples. "I'm starting to get a headache."

Chuck walked over and started banging on the steel door. "Hey, anybody down there?" he shouted. "Patrick?"

The noise startled Bella, who began to cry.

"Shhh," Natalie whispered to her as she moved toward the open doorway between the pantry and kitchen. "You're all right. Hush now."

Bella's cries quieted almost immediately. Chuck didn't bang on the door again, but he put his mouth near it as he called out again. "Patrick? Can you hear me?"

They all waited in silence for some response but none came. Chuck turned to the group. "I don't think he's down there."

"Or if he is down there, he's in no shape to talk," Vonnie said. "We've got to find the key or figure out some way to open that door."

"That door is solid steel." Chuck massaged his knuckles.

"I know a way." Levi hurried out of the pantry.

A moment later, Sarah heard the sound of the screened porch door banging shut. She slipped out of the pantry in time to watch Levi through the window as he disappeared inside the shed. She hoped he'd remembered where to find a spare padlock key in there, but when he returned to the inn he had an axe in his hands.

"Everybody stand back," Levi warned as he made his way to the cellar door. The pantry emptied, everyone gathered around the open doorway as Levi swung the ax at the heavy padlock. The grinding noise of metal on metal made Sarah's teeth hurt, but the blow barely caused a dent in the padlock or the door.

He swung again and again, until Finn finally grabbed the axe handle and pulled it out of his hands. "This isn't going to work."

"It's got to work," Levi said, gasping for breath. "Patrick has to be down there! There's nowhere else he could be."

"If he is down there, we'll have to find another way to get him out." Finn ushered Levi out of the pantry and back to the door to the screened porch. Sarah watched him hand the axe back to Levi and lower his voice.

"Now put this back in the shed. The last thing we need is easy access to a deadly weapon."

Levi turned around without a word and headed for the shed. When Finn saw Sarah watching, he asked, "What shall we try next? A pipe bomb?"

She sighed, so frustrated by that locked cellar door she felt like kicking it down herself. "Don't tempt me."

When they walked into the kitchen, the savory aroma of bacon made Sarah's stomach rumble. She knew she should eat something. Otherwise, the girls might refuse to eat too, and they all needed to keep up their strength during this stressful time. But she didn't want to stop looking for Patrick.

"Breakfast is just about ready," Vonnie announced. "Go ahead and sit down at the table."

Sarah set out sweet rolls and orange juice, filled with too much nervous energy to sit down yet. Dorothy poured coffee while the twins set plates, glasses, and silverware on the dining room table.

A few moments later, they all sat down to Vonnie's breakfast of scrambled eggs and bacon. For several moments, the only sound in the room was the clink of silverware against the plates.

Natalie held the baby in her lap while she ate, alternately feeding herself and Bella. "Thank you for cooking us breakfast, Vonnie."

"You're welcome."

Sarah glanced at the twins, who both picked at their scrambled eggs. Amy kept looking across the table at Finn while Audrey sat next to Natalie and tickled Bella's chin. The baby giggled, a small bubble forming on her lips.

Sarah looked across the table at Levi. He sat hunched over his food, one arm circling around the top of his plate. He shoveled the food into his mouth so fast she wondered if he even had time to taste it.

Dorothy finished eating first, pushing her half-finished plate away from her. Then she picked up her coffee cup and took a dainty sip. "You know," she said, setting her cup back on the saucer, "this might be a good time to formally introduce ourselves."

Chuck groaned. "Do we have to?"

Dorothy blushed. "Well, of course not. I just thought. . . . "

"I think it's a good idea," Vonnie said, casting a warning glance up at her husband. "Seems like one of us is—that is, we're going to be stuck here together for a while. We might as well get to know each other a little."

Chuck nodded and looked over at Dorothy. "Why don't you go first?"

Dorothy cleared her throat. "Well, I'm Dorothy Ogden, from Schenectady, New York."

"And I'm Natalie Minnick, from Concord, New Hampshire." She turned her baby around to face the group. "And this is Bella. She's six months old."

Audrey was next in line at the table and she looked over at Sarah, who nodded her head in approval.

"I'm Audrey Hart," she said, "from Maple Hill, Massachusetts."

"And I'm Sarah Hart, also from Maple Hill." She felt like she should say something more, but the tension in the air wasn't conducive to conversation. Everyone looked uncomfortable except Bella, who was gumming a cracker.

"And I'm Amy Hart, Audrey's twin, so I'm obviously from Maple Hill too."

"Chuck and I are from Providence, Rhode Island," Vonnie said and pushed the bowl of scrambled eggs toward Levi. "Please help yourself to more food."

Levi took her up on the offer, scraping the last of the eggs onto his plate. "Levi Prince. Hartford."

"Finn Hawkins, New York City," Finn said, reaching for his coffee cup. "I'd give anything to be there right now."

They sat at the table in silence, the only sounds the ticking of the grandfather clock in the corner of the dining room and the wind howling outside. Even the baby seemed to sense the mood, jawing on the cracker but not making a noise.

At last, Sarah spoke. "Maybe we should go over everything that we remember from last night. That might help us figure out what happened."

"I'm game," Finn said.

"Then tell us how you got that shiner," Levi said to him.

Finn plucked at his sweater. "I hit my face on the bathroom door last night when I was getting ready for bed. I'm blind as a bat once I take my contact lenses out."

Sarah eyed him skeptically and turned to Chuck. "Did you notice anything unusual last night?"

He looked over at Bella. "Just the baby crying for an hour or so."

Natalie shifted in her chair. "She had a touch of colic. It wasn't that long."

"You're right. I don't think it was an hour," Sarah gently concurred. "I heard the baby too, but the crying only lasted thirty minutes or so."

"I'm sorry," Natalie said. "I'm doing the best I can. It's not easy, you know."

"We're not blaming you, dear," Dorothy assured her. "And it certainly has nothing to do with what happened to Patrick."

"Everything was fine when I left here last night," Levi blurted.

None of the three men had admitted to scuffling with Patrick in the parlor, unaware Sarah had witnessed part of it. She didn't intend to ask them yet, hoping one of them might accidentally reveal something.

Finn rose from his chair and walked over to the window, staring out at the white landscape. "I'm supposed to be at an important meeting in Hartford today. Guess that's cancelled."

Until that moment, Sarah had completely forgotten about the quilting workshop she was supposed to attend that day. Finding Patrick had taken precedence over everything else in her mind. Until they found a way into that cellar, she needed to figure out who might have assaulted him—before that person struck again.

 CHAPTER FIVE

After breakfast, they all headed for the parlor. Sarah stopped just long enough to check the landline phone on the front desk, but the line was still dead.

When they reached the parlor, Finn Hawkins and Chuck walked over to pick up the crushed red velvet settee that had been overturned when Vonnie suddenly shouted, "Stop!"

Chuck looked over at his wife. "What in the world are you hollering about?"

"Maybe we shouldn't touch anything." Vonnie twisted her thin hands together. "On all the police shows, you're never supposed to touch anything in the crime scene. We could be destroying evidence."

Chuck reached for the scrolled arm of the settee. "Don't be silly, Von. We need some place to sit until they dig us out of this snow."

"Vonnie has a point," Sarah said. "We should take pictures so the police will know how the parlor looked before we put all the furniture back in place."

Finn stepped back, annoyance etched on his face. He'd left it unshaven, but had changed from his suit into a pair of blue jeans and a green crewneck sweater. "Anybody have a camera handy?"

Audrey held up her cell phone.

"Perfect," Sarah exclaimed, proud of her granddaughter's quick thinking.

Amy moved toward the staircase. "I can go get my camera too. I left it up in our room."

Sarah reached out and grabbed her arm. "We're sticking together, remember? Nobody goes anywhere alone."

Amy nodded and muttered, "Sorry, Grandma."

Dorothy nodded. "I think that's a rule we should all follow until we get to the bottom of this mess. We can't trust anyone."

Natalie stepped forward, her baby on her shoulder. "You really think one of us is responsible for . . . this?" She pointed to the blood on the floor and cast a wary gaze at the people around her.

"I'd say it's likely," Chuck replied. "Either one of us—or Patrick."

"What about an intruder?" Dorothy ventured. "Someone could have broken in while we were asleep."

"You heard him." Chuck pointed at Levi, "Nobody else could get in or out of this place in this weather. Both doors were locked and there are no signs of a break-in. If there are only two keys to the inn that means someone here has to be responsible."

"And that's why it's smart for us to stick together," Sarah added. "There's safety in numbers."

Finn arched a brow. "What about tonight? I'm too old for slumber parties."

"So am I," Dorothy said dryly. "I think if we all go to bed at the same time and lock our doors, we should be safe."

Vonnie nodded. "I'm not only going to lock our door, I'm going to barricade it with the dresser." She looked around the room. "So if anyone tries to break in, we'll hear him coming."

Finn reached for Audrey's phone. "Let's just get these pictures taken so we can sit down." He began pushing buttons on the phone, trying to figure out how to take a photo.

"Do you know what you're doing?" Audrey questioned skeptically.

Finn glanced at her uncertainly and then grinned as the phone's camera app flashed on the LCD screen.

Sarah watched Finn take photographs from all different angles in the parlor. When she'd invited Amy and Audrey to spend the weekend with her she'd never imagined they'd find themselves in the middle of a mystery. She just prayed that this mystery would resolve itself quickly; the girls were too young to witness a tragic story unfold.

"There," Finn said, handing the camera back to Audrey. "Now are there any other objections or can we start moving furniture?"

"We'll all pitch in." Sarah pushed up her sleeves, then reached for the framed needlepoint that had fallen off the wall. The initials M.R.G. were embroidered at the bottom—Patrick's grandmother's initials. Sarah carefully hung the framed needlework back on the wall, praying that Maeve's grandson was still alive.

Her gaze moved to the parlor window, the snow still falling heavily outside. The wind had picked up again too, creating drifts almost as high as the windowsill. She thought there was a good chance they'd be stranded here overnight.

Her thoughts were interrupted by Finn. "I'm gonna go have a smoke outside," he said.

Vonnie looked up from the table where she sat huddled with Chuck. "Out in that blizzard?"

"I really need a smoke." He pulled a pack of cigarettes out of his pocket. "Unless you want me to light up right here?"

Natalie jumped to her feet. "Around my baby?"

"That's why I'm going outside."

Levi leaned forward where he was perched on the settee, his elbows on his knees. "I'm not sure that's a good idea."

"I appreciate your concern," Finn said dryly, "but I'll be fine."

"I'm not concerned for you," Levi said.

Finn blinked. "Yeah, I've got a secret plan." He held up the cigarette pack in his hand. "I've got the weapon hidden in here and I'm going to bury it next to the mailbox."

"I don't think anyone should go outside." Chuck scratched the gray stubble on his chin.

"Then you leave me no choice." Finn drew a cigarette out of the pack, and flicked his lighter.

"How about the screened porch?" Sarah suggested before Finn could light his cigarette. She walked over to him. "The smoke won't drift through the rest of the house and you won't get lost in a snowdrift."

"Wait a minute," Natalie said, concern etched on her face. "You said we were supposed to all stick together."

"I know." Sarah said, torn between adhering to the rule and making it more practical. "But we've searched the inn as best as we can, so we know there's no one here but us."

"Except the cellar," Vonnie said.

"That's right." Sarah looked around the room. "We'll all still be safe if only one person is missing from the room at a time. Or in my case, my granddaughters and me."

"Might keep some of us from going stir-crazy," Finn said, glancing at Chuck.

Sarah saw Chuck flush, but he didn't say anything. "So are we agreed?"

"Agreed," everyone said in unison.

"Sounds like a good compromise to me," Dorothy set her knitting bag on the table beside her and kneaded her fingers together.

The rest of the group nodded, all except Finn. She wondered why he was so eager to go outside in this blizzard. She hadn't smelled smoke on him before, but her nose wasn't as sensitive to odors as it used to be. Perhaps Levi was right that

Finn was using it as an excuse. Then again, Finn did have a pack of cigarettes on him.

"Fine," Finn said, turned on his heel and strode out of the parlor.

Everyone seemed at a loss for what to do next. They all wandered around the parlor and library, not really settling on any activity. Sarah walked over to the window and parted the curtain.

The snow continued to fall, the wind blowing it into huge drifts that threatened to bury them. Then she thought she saw something moving in the storm. She rubbed the frost off the windowpane, and leaned closer for a better look. She could just barely make out the figure of a man near the corner of the house. It was too far away for her to see his face, but she recognized the coat and hat.

It was Finn. He was walking toward the shed.

CHAPTER SIX

Do you think cabin fever is setting in?" Dorothy asked the group. She walked closer to the table where Chuck and Vonnie sat. "Mr. Hawkins seemed pretty agitated."

Sarah turned from the window but positioned herself so she could see Finn when he left the shed.

"Well, I'm no expert by any means," Vonnie said. "But addictions like nicotine can cause anger issues and anger can lead to violence...."

Sarah looked at Chuck. He sat quietly by his wife, letting her do all the talking.

Natalie cast a nervous glance in the direction of the screened porch. "But do you really think he's capable of hurting someone?"

"I think so," Amy exclaimed from her perch in the library. She jumped off the window seat and joined them in the parlor.

Sarah was glad to see Amy showing enthusiasm, but didn't want to join her granddaughter in her speculation. She was eager to hear what the other guests had to say, and was hoping one of them might reveal a nugget or two of information that would help her solve this case.

"Well, I don't think we should jump to conclusions until we have all the facts," Audrey said primly. "Isn't that right, Grandma?"

Sarah nodded.

Amy stared down her sister. "Does this mean you like Mr. Hawkins?"

"I never said I liked him," Audrey replied, turning her attention to the baby. "But wouldn't a guilty person want to be less conspicuous so people wouldn't suspect him?"

She had a point, Sarah thought. And she couldn't help but like Finn and his sharp-witted comments.

Vonnie leaned forward and lowered her voice. "Well, I'm not ready to convict him or anything. I'm just saying that Finn seems like the type who could do something like that."

"He's big enough to have done it," Levi said. "Taller than Patrick, anyway."

Sarah watched their faces. If Finn wasn't guilty, then the real culprit was probably enjoying this—maybe even fueling the fire. Vonnie had broached the subject first and been supported by both Levi and Natalie. Neither Chuck nor Dorothy had said anything yet. Would the real culprit join in, or stay quiet for fear of saying something incriminating?

"Size and strength might not matter if the culprit caught Patrick unaware," Dorothy said, breaking her silence. "He—or she—could have snuck up behind him and knocked him unconscious."

"But they'd have to be strong enough to drag the body away," Vonnie pointed out.

"And smart enough to hide all the evidence." Natalie pointed to Finn's briefcase. "He's probably a lawyer or something."

"And his black eye?" Levi whispered, glancing over his shoulder to make sure Finn wasn't approaching.

Natalie agreed. "Running into a door? I mean, come on. At least be a little creative."

As they built a case against Finn, Sarah wondered about the clothes he'd been wearing this morning. Unless he was a quick-change artist, he wouldn't have had time to change into his suit after hearing Dorothy's screams. Had he slept in his clothes?

Or never gone to bed at all?

But Sarah needed more than a black eye, a wrinkled suit, and a personality to prove her case. She needed to know why Finn Hawkins would want to hurt Patrick.

Until then, everyone at the inn remained on the suspect list.

She finally saw Finn emerge from the shed. He carried a shovel and began clearing the narrow walk between the shed and the screened porch. Was that all he had gone to the shed for?

When Finn finally returned to the parlor, no one said a word to him. He settled back in a chair and started working on some paperwork.

"Now. How are we going to get into that cellar?" Sarah asked aloud.

Chuck shook his head. "There's no way we can break through that steel door."

"We don't even know for sure if Patrick's down there," Natalie said. She sat on the floor, Bella playing on a pink flannel baby blanket beside her.

"Where else could he be?" Vonnie asked. "We've looked everywhere."

Finn got up and paced back and forth in front of the window. "He could have taken off somewhere last night."

"Without his keys or wallet?" Dorothy said. "I think that's highly unlikely."

Finn turned around. "Maybe he went outside for a walk and accidentally locked himself out of the house."

"But the dead bolts were turned." Sarah noted. "He couldn't lock himself out without his key." Another thought occurred to her. Maybe there were more than two keys to the inn. She only had Levi's word on that, and she certainly considered him a suspect since he had still been working last night when she went to bed. She had no way of knowing if he'd even returned to his home in Hartford as he'd claimed.

She looked over at Levi. ""What time did you leave last night?"

He thought for a moment. "Sometime after midnight, I guess. My shift usually ends at eleven, but Patrick had a bunch of extra chores for me to do."

Sarah let that information sink in, remembering how irritated Patrick had seemed with Levi. As more possibilities filled her mind, she realized she needed to write them down in one of her notebooks to keep everything straight.

"I need to get some things from my room." She turned to the twins. "Why don't you two come upstairs with me? You can take a book or your sketchbook to keep you busy today."

Sarah and the girls left the parlor and returned to their rooms. Audrey grabbed her sketchbook and charcoal pencil while Amy retrieved her book and MP3 player with headphones. Sarah dug through her suitcase looking for a notebook.

Sketchbook in hand, Audrey walked over and sat on the edge of Sarah's bed. "It's weird thinking one of the people downstairs isn't who they say they are. They all seem so nice."

A flashing light in Sarah's purse caught her attention. She picked up her cell phone, surprised to see a new text message there. "Well, what do you know." She held up the phone to show the girls. "Looks like a message got through. Maybe we have reception again."

"Who's it from?" Audrey asked.

Sarah pressed a button on the phone to read the text message. "Martha. It says 'Call me ASAP.'"

ASAP? Martha didn't say that often. And Sarah didn't know who else might be trying to call her—the Bradford Manor nurses, maybe, if something was wrong with her father. She hoped they'd call Jason—William's second emergency contact—if they couldn't reach her. But that didn't help ease her worry any. She hated the thought of not being there for her father if something had happened.

"See if you can call her back," Audrey said, pulling her own cell phone from her pocket.

Amy scampered for her room. "I'm going to get my phone too."

Sarah dialed Martha's number and waited but nothing happened. Then she tried texting her. A moment later, a red X appeared on her phone, indicating that the message hadn't gone through. "My phone still isn't getting reception."

"Neither is mine," Audrey said as her sister walked back into the room. "I was really hoping I could text my friends today."

"Me too," Amy said, staring mournfully at her cell phone.

"Well, one message got through," Sarah reminded them, "so they might work later."

Amy slipped her phone into her pocket. "I hope so."

As they headed back downstairs, Sarah didn't like knowing her ninety-seven-year-old father might need her and she couldn't be reached.

Or the message might not even be about her dad. The text message could be about anything. Although Martha knew she was away for the weekend, so she wouldn't send a message like that unless it was important. Maybe something had happened to Ernie. Sarah sent up a small prayer for Martha, that whatever was so urgent would be okay.

When they returned to the parlor, Sarah noticed that everyone had separated. Vonnie and Chuck stood whispering by the ficus tree, Levi and Dorothy were seated near the window, and Finn was pacing back and forth in the library.

Only Natalie was in the same spot on the floor and she stood up when she saw Sarah and the girls.

"I need to go upstairs now to get some more diapers and a bottle for Bella," Natalie said, reaching for the baby.

Audrey stepped toward her. "Do you want me to watch her for you while you're gone?"

Natalie hesitated for a moment and then said, "That would be great." She handed the baby over to her. "You be good for Audrey, Bella. Momma will be right back."

Bella cooed at her mother and watched her walk toward the doorway. As soon as Natalie was out of sight, the baby began to cry.

Audrey looked helplessly at Sarah. "Grandma, what do I do now?"

"Try to distract her," Sarah said, walking over to them. "Talk to her."

"What do I say?"

"Anything," Sarah said with a smile. "Just make eye contact and sound happy."

Audrey held up the baby so she could see her face. "Hey, Bella. Hey, girl, it's all right. We're going to have so much fun today."

Bella's cries turned into muted sniffles. Then she blinked up at Audrey and her mouth bloomed into a smile.

Audrey laughed as she looked over at Sarah. "It's working."

"Can I hold her?" Amy said, reaching out to Bella.

"Maybe in a little while," Sarah said. "Audrey's just got her settled down."

"You're such a cute little thing," Audrey cooed.

By the time Natalie returned, Bella was laughing at the silly faces Audrey was making.

"Thanks for watching her," Natalie told her. "You must babysit a lot."

"No, but we did take a babysitting course," Audrey admitted.

"Well, you're really good with kids."

"I'm going to read my book in the library," Amy said to Sarah.

"Okay," Sarah told her, and watched as Amy settled back into the window seat.

When she glanced over at Audrey, Sarah saw she was still occupied with the baby. This gave her the perfect opportunity to start compiling what she knew about the mystery so far.

She sat down in a wing chair near the fire, opened her notebook and wrote down the names of everyone in the house and what she knew about them.

Levi – Hartford, CT. Employed by Patrick. Claims he drove to work Saturday morning and got caught in the blizzard. But blizzard would have started before he left for work. Has the only other key to the inn. He says the backdoor was locked when he arrived.

Finn Hawkins – New York, NY. Wanted to talk to Patrick in private the night before he disappeared. Now has a black eye. Was wearing the same suit from the night before when Dorothy's screams brought everyone to the parlor.

Dorothy Ogden – Schenectady, NY. Said Patrick told her she could use the kitchen whenever she wanted to make tea. She found the mess in the parlor early Saturday morning.

Natalie Minnick – Concord, NH. Single mother with six-month-old baby. Bella cried for a good half hour during the night Patrick disappeared. Was Natalie out of her room during that time?

Chuck and Vonnie Thayer – Providence, RI. Married couple. Vonnie worked as a nurse's aide. Chuck gets violent when upset—broke bottles in the shed.

Sarah sat back and studied the list and realized she was missing someone.

Patrick Maguire – Hartford, CT. Owner of the Red Clover Inn. He seemed to have problems with Levi and Finn the night of his disappearance. Also scuffled with a man in the parlor. His keys and wallet are still in his room. Acted a little tipsy the night he disappeared.

One of the people on her list was responsible for the blood in the parlor. Now she just had to figure out which one.

She decided to talk with Dorothy first. The older woman had already separated herself from Levi, who now lay sleeping on the settee, and had settled into a chair by the window with her knitting basket.

As Sarah passed by the library she could see Amy still lying with her book in the window seat. She wasn't worried about her granddaughter overhearing bits and pieces of their conversation as long as the other guests weren't able to eavesdrop.

"What are you making?" Sarah asked as she took a seat beside Dorothy.

"A baby sweater for Bella. I didn't have any baby yarn with me, but this is a nice, soft sock yarn, so I think it will work."

"Do you knit a lot of baby clothes?"

"No," Dorothy said. "My husband and I—we were never able to have children." Dorothy's voice softened. "My Leo passed away last year."

"Oh, I'm so sorry."

Dorothy kept her gaze on her knitting. "We had a good life together, even without kids. We traveled a lot and had some wonderful adventures."

"I lost my husband Gerry five years ago," Sarah told her. "The happy memories help, don't they?"

Dorothy nodded. "They do."

They both grew quiet and Sarah found herself staring out the window, her mind on some of those happy memories. They'd built a snowman together the first year they were married and named him Frank. They'd decorated him with Gerry's old clothes and tossed snowballs at each other. Then they'd warmed up by the fireplace, snuggling together on the sofa and talking.

The steady click of Dorothy's knitting needles brought her back to the present.

"Doesn't knitting bother your fingers?" she asked, remembering Dorothy's arthritis.

"A little, but it helps keep them nimble."

The conversation lulled again and Sarah struggled for something to say. "You've got the perfect guest room for a cold day like this. It reminds me of summer."

"It *is* nice."

"So what brought you to the Red Clover Inn? Have you been here before?"

Dorothy paused. "No, I heard about it from a friend."

"Have you traveled much since...?" Out of the corner of her eye, Sarah saw Finn stop his pacing in front of the fireplace and sit down to do some work.

"No. This sounded like a good place to get my feet wet again." She looked outside. "Although I wasn't planning on quite this much precipitation."

"I think the winter storm caught most of us by surprise."

"I don't really mind. Since I retired, I don't have any place I have to be."

"What kind of work did you do?" Sarah asked.

Dorothy took a moment to count a stitch and said, "I was a financial advisor."

"Did you work in a bank?"

Dorothy smiled. "Several different banks, actually. The job isn't everyone's cup of tea, but I really enjoyed it."

"And you're from Schenectady?"

"Born and raised there. I used to go fishing in the Mohawk River all the time when I was a girl."

"My husband liked to fish too."

The conversation ran out of steam, but Sarah intended to write down every word, no matter how insignificant it seemed. Whenever she restored a quilt, she took care to trace every thread before she cut it, not wanting to unravel the whole thing. Solving a mystery took the same kind of care.

Sarah resumed her seat by the fire to record all the new information in her notebook. She wrote down every detail, no matter how small.

None of it fit together in any meaningful way yet, but just as with quilt making, she simply needed more pieces before she could begin to see a pattern.

She looked over at Amy, noting that she'd not said a word for a while. Sarah set down her notebook and walked into the library. "How's it going?"

"Fine."

"You've been awfully quiet. Is anything wrong?"

"No, I just really like this book."

Sarah knew what it was like to get lost in a good book.

orothy picked up her knitting basket. "I need to go to my room to freshen up."

Sarah had a hard time imagining the diminutive septuagenarian engaging in a struggle with Patrick and coming out the winner. Doing so with arthritis would make it nearly impossible. And she'd been the one to discover the crime, which didn't prove her innocence, but made her appear more like a victim than a perpetrator. But she was a suspect, just like everyone else.

Sarah turned to a fresh sheet of paper in her notebook, deciding to make a log every time someone left the parlor, along with noting how long they were gone and the reason they gave for leaving. It would help her keep track of everyone and provide a detailed timeline of events in case anything else suspicious happened.

Audrey walked over to her chair. "Grandma, I don't feel good."

"What's wrong?" Sarah asked, her hand moving automatically to the girl's forehead.

"My stomach hurts."

Audrey didn't feel feverish to Sarah and she certainly hadn't been acting sick. Sarah wondered if some of the tension in the room was starting to affect her. "Where exactly does it hurt?"

Audrey circled a hand around her stomach. "Kind of all over."

"Why don't you lie down on that love seat for a little while," Sarah suggested.

"But I'm not tired."

"I know, but a little rest might help your stomach feel better."

Audrey grimaced, but to Sarah's surprise, she didn't try to argue anymore. She walked over to the love seat and lay down, tucking one of the tapestry pillows under her head before closing her eyes.

"You seem like such a good grandma." Natalie moved herself and Bella closer to Sarah. "How do you always know what to say and do?"

Sarah laughed. "I don't. Believe me, I've made plenty of mistakes in my time."

"Really?" Natalie looked down at her daughter. "I feel like I've made a ton of mistakes with Bella already. And she's only six months old!"

Natalie was an attractive girl, with soft, auburn hair and bright green eyes. She was awfully thin, though. Sarah wondered if she spent so much time taking care of her baby that she didn't take good care of herself.

Now that she thought about it, Natalie hadn't eaten much at breakfast. She'd filled her plate, but mostly moved the food around, eating only a few bites. At the time, she'd assumed Natalie had lost her appetite because of Patrick's disappearance and the bloody parlor. Now she wondered if there were other problems weighing on the girl's mind.

"What kind of mistakes?" Sarah asked softly.

Natalie shrugged. "Oh you know, the usual."

Sarah tried to be encouraging. "Bella seems happy today. We've barely heard a peep out of her."

Natalie smiled down at her child. "She's always happy."

"Except for a little while last night?"

Natalie kept her gaze on Bella. "I said she just had a touch of colic."

"Well, I'm glad it doesn't seem to be bothering her today."

"Me too."

The silence stretched between them while Natalie played with her baby.

"I remember when my babies would cry in the middle of the night. I'd jump right out of bed while my husband stayed sound asleep. I guess I'm still sensitive to the sound."

"Sorry if she kept you up."

"You have nothing to be sorry about. Babies cry all the time."

Natalie looked up at Sarah. "Well, somebody told me that you shouldn't pick babies up when they cry at night or…or…they get spoiled. So I let her cry until I just couldn't stand it anymore."

Sarah nodded, noting the flush in Natalie's cheeks. "Motherhood is a learn-as-you-go job. Does Bella ever stay with her father?"

"No." Natalie straightened a corner of the pink blanket. Sarah's heart went out to the girl, imagining how hard it would be to raise a child on one's own. She hadn't been the perfect mother to Jason and Jenna, but she and Gerry had done their best as parents. Sharing both the pleasure and pain of child rearing had helped them grow closer. She could always brag about her children to her husband, knowing he shared her unconditional love and pride.

"Do you have anyone to help you?" Sarah asked.

Natalie shook her head. "Not really. My mother passed away just a couple of months after Bella was born." Her voice caught and she paused a few moments before continuing. "Would you like to see a picture of her?"

"I'd love to."

Natalie dug into her bag until she pulled out a photograph. "This is my mom at Bella's christening."

Sarah studied the thin woman in the photo. Her face was gaunt, but her smile was full and lovely as she gazed down at her granddaughter. The baby wore a lace christening gown and looked like an angel.

"They're both beautiful and she looks so proud of her granddaughter."

"She was," Natalie said wistfully. "Bella's wearing the same gown that I wore at my christening and my father wore at his."

Sarah handed the photo back to Natalie. "What a wonderful keepsake—both the gown and the picture."

Natalie placed the photograph back in her bag. "Well, I came to Hartford to get a fresh start."

"How did you pick Hartford?"

Natalie shrugged. "A friend of mine works at a day care center and said she could get me a job there. Then Bella and I could be together while I work."

"That sounds like a good plan."

"Yeah, I just hope I can make it to my interview on Monday." She glanced toward the window. "We'll be out of here by then, won't we?"

"I hope so." They'd only been snowbound for a few hours, but it seemed much longer to Sarah. Probably to Patrick, too, if he was still alive.

If only she could find a way into that cellar.

She turned her attention back to Natalie. Despite her compassion for the girl's circumstances, there were a few things about her situation that seemed a little odd. Like how a single mother without a job could afford a room at the Red Clover Inn.

Sarah studied her face. "So what made you decide to stay here?"

"My friend recommended it."

Sarah watched Bella scoot on her stomach. "It's too bad you couldn't have stayed with your friend and saved some money. This place is very nice, but it's a little pricey."

Natalie hesitated. "Well, I found a coupon on the Red Clover Inn Web site that offered two nights for the price of one, so it wasn't too bad."

"Really?" Sarah noted that Natalie was still looking at Bella instead of her. She hadn't seen any coupons on the Web site when she'd made her reservations. "Lucky you."

"I know." Natalie picked up the baby and cradled her in her arms. "My friend did invite me to stay with her, but I didn't want to impose after all she's doing for me. Especially with Bella being a little colicky."

"Well, I hope you get the job," Sarah said sincerely. Whatever Natalie's story, it was clear she dearly loved her daughter.

Natalie flashed a smile in her direction. "Thanks. I hope so too."

Dorothy returned to the parlor carrying a cup of hot tea. She'd obviously taken a detour into the kitchen on the way back from her bedroom. Sarah wrote that fact down in her notebook, along with the information she'd learned about Natalie and her baby.

"Bella's probably getting hungry," Natalie said when she saw Dorothy. "I'm going to warm up a bottle for her."

"Do you want me to watch her while you do that?" Sarah offered.

Before Natalie could reply, Audrey popped off the love seat. "I can watch her."

"Are you sure you feel well enough?" Sarah asked. "I can watch her if you want to rest some more."

"I'm sure."

Sarah looked over at Amy, who still lounged in the window seat in the library. Amy was watching them, but when she met Sarah's gaze, she turned her attention back to her book.

Twenty minutes later, Natalie returned with Bella's bottle, claiming it had taken so long because she couldn't figure out how to work the microwave. She took the baby from Audrey.

After Natalie sat down in the Windsor rocking chair and began feeding Bella, Chuck and Vonnie headed out of the parlor.

"We're going to walk around a bit and stretch our legs," Vonnie explained. "Chuck's knees get stiff if we sit too long."

"I thought I'd pound on that cellar door again," Chuck said. "Maybe Patrick was asleep last time or something and didn't hear me before."

Sarah nodded, intending to do the same thing herself the next time she left the parlor. They couldn't stop looking for Patrick, even if their initial search had failed. The thought of him hurt and bleeding made her heart ache.

The mantle clock ticked above the fireplace as everyone busied themselves. Dorothy started knitting a sleeve, Finn had buried himself in a report, and Levi was playing a board game with Audrey.

Sarah watched them all for a long moment and returned to her notes, wondering what her next step should be. She still needed to interview Finn, Chuck, Vonnie, and Levi.

"Grandma?"

Sarah looked up from her notebook to see Amy standing in front of her. "Yes, dear?"

"I'm done with my book. Can I go upstairs and get another one?"

"We can't leave the parlor while Chuck and Vonnie are gone. Are there any books in the library you'd like to read until they get back?"

"I don't want to read those. They're like a thousand years old."

"Well, some of those old books are pretty good." Sarah started to rise out of her chair. "Do you want me to help you pick one out?"

"No," Amy replied. "I want to read one of the books I brought with me."

Sarah sighed as she sat back down. The girl could be just as stubborn as her father. "All right. Then you'll have to wait until the Thayers get back. It shouldn't be long."

"Okay," Amy said, returning to her perch in the library.

To Sarah's chagrin, Chuck and Vonnie didn't return for almost half an hour. She was beginning to worry about them when they finally walked into the parlor.

"Sorry we took so long," Chuck said, reaching down to rub his leg. "My hip started bothering me so we had to sit a spell." She watched him walk back to the table where he and Vonnie had set up camp but didn't notice a limp in his step.

"Did you hear anything from the cellar?"

Chuck took a moment to answer. "Um…no. Not a thing."

Sarah rose from her chair and called for Audrey. "Amy and I are going upstairs. Why don't you come with us?"

"Go ahead," Levi told her. "We can finish the game later."

Audrey bounced over to them. "What are we going to do?"

"Amy needs another book," Sarah said, tucking her notebook under her arm. She couldn't imagine what Chuck and Vonnie had been doing all that time.

Just one more detail to add to her notebook.

"Let's stop by the kitchen first," Sarah said as they passed by the front desk. She paused for a moment to check the phone, but the line was still dead.

The girls followed Sarah through the kitchen and into the pantry.

"Do you think Patrick's down there?" Audrey asked as Sarah approached the locked cellar door.

"I don't know where else he could be." Sarah reached up to pound on the door with her fist. "Patrick? Patrick, are you there?"

The girls pounded on the door with her and then they all stopped and listened, hoping to hear some sound from the other side.

Nothing.

With a sigh of disappointment, Sarah studied the door from top to bottom. The hinges looked impenetrable and there seemed to be no way to unfasten them. At last, she ushered the girls out of the pantry and headed for the stairs.

When they reached their rooms, Amy retrieved her book while Sarah checked her cell phone to see if she'd received any more texts or calls. There were none, and when she tried to dial out, the screen on her phone read: Out of Service. She read Martha's text again, the urgency of it still bothering her.

"What's wrong, Grandma?" Audrey asked as she walked into her room.

Sarah looked up from her phone. "Oh nothing. I'm fine. How are you feeling?"

Audrey placed a hand over her stomach. "Still a little icky."

Sarah chuckled. "That's a word I haven't heard in a while. Your aunt Jenna used to say it all the time."

"She did?"

Sarah nodded. "She thought snakes were icky and lima beans were icky. But do you know what she considered the ickiest thing of all?"

Audrey's blue eyes grew round with curiosity. "What?"

"Your dad."

Audrey giggled as she settled onto the bed next to Sarah. "Really? Why would she think that?"

"Well, Jenna was four years younger than your dad and he did like to boss her around."

"He can be kind of bossy."

"Sometimes she'd get so mad that she'd hide somewhere all day just so he couldn't find her." Sarah smiled at the memory. "It used to drive Jason crazy."

"Where did she hide?"

"Well, let me think." Sarah pictured her little eight-year-old Jenna with blonde pigtails. "One time I found her hiding in the back of my closet. Another time she was downstairs in Grandpa Gerry's woodshop, hiding behind a big sheet of plywood. Then there was the time she hid someplace Jason never thought of looking."

"Where?"

"In his room under his bed."

Audrey leaned back against a pillow. "Didn't she ever get tired of hiding?"

"Not for a long time. Not until she was about ten years old. Then something happened that made her promise never to hide anywhere again."

Audrey's eyes widened. "What?"

"I'll tell you later," Sarah said as Amy walked into the room. Sarah thought it might be good to leave a cliff-hanger for Audrey to think about. Maybe that would take her mind off what was happening at the inn, especially since Sarah believed the girl's stomach problems were probably caused by stress rather than illness.

"What's going on?" Amy asked, a thick book tucked under her arm.

"Nothing." Audrey jumped off the bed. "I can't believe it took you that long to pick out a silly book. How many did you bring?"

"Six." Amy looked up at Sarah. "I never know which one I'll feel like reading."

"That sounds reasonable to me." Sarah smiled at Amy as she moved to the door. "Shall we go back downstairs?"

"Sure," Amy said, leading the way to the door. "The sooner we get back there, the sooner we can figure out what happened to Mr. Maguire."

 ## CHAPTER EIGHT

W hen they returned to the parlor, Sarah realized what she had to do next. She surveyed the room—Dorothy was still knitting by the window, now working on the second sleeve of the baby sweater; Chuck and Vonnie were sitting with their heads together at the game table while Finn paced back and forth in front of the fireplace again; Natalie still sat in the rocking chair, her head tilted to one side as both she and the baby napped. Sarah approached Levi, who was standing in the library searching the shelves.

"What are you looking for?"

He turned to her. "I thought there might be some blueprints of the inn in here that would help us find Patrick. You know, like showing a different way into the cellar or something."

"Any luck?"

He shook his head. "Not yet."

Sarah knew she could help him search, but she hoped her idea would be more fruitful. "I need the extra key to Patrick's room."

Levi blinked. "What for?"

"I want to take another look at it," she said, not bothering to lower her voice. She wanted to see if anyone reacted to her request. "There might be a clue that we missed the first time around."

"Like what?" Vonnie appeared beneath the wide arch separating the parlor from the library.

"I don't know," Sarah told her honestly.

Vonnie exchanged glances with her husband. "Well, I'm not sure you should be traipsing around in there. I mean, he may be missing, but it's still his room."

Finn arched a brow. "You think Sarah's going to steal from him?"

Vonnie blushed. "I never said that. It just seems... strange to me."

"What's strange is that Patrick is still missing," Finn replied. "Unless you're ready to give up looking for him."

"Now hold on there, Hawkins," Chuck said, rising from the table. His first step hitched a little as he moved forward. "Vonnie means well. She's as concerned about Patrick as the rest of us."

"That's right," Vonnie said. "When we do find him, he may not be happy about the fact that people were waltzing in and out of his room."

"That brings up another subject," Dorothy said from her chair, her gaze on her knitting. "I don't really feel comfortable knowing there's an extra key to my room floating around here."

"Who do you think is going to use it?" Levi asked her.

Dorothy tugged at the ball of pink yarn in her knitting basket. "Maybe the same person who hurt Patrick. That's exactly my point. We have no idea who might use one of those extra keys or when."

"That's why we're barricading our door," Vonnie said. "Although I wouldn't mind having the second key to our room for safekeeping."

Natalie stirred in the rocking chair. "What are we talking about?"

"Whether those extra room keys should stay at the front desk," Dorothy informed her. "I personally don't think it's very safe."

"I'm sure they're locked up in a drawer." Finn looked over at Levi. "Of course, only one person here has the key to that drawer."

"Actually, I don't," Levi said. "Patrick is the only one who has the master key."

Sarah stared at him, his words making her uneasy. "You mean the drawer with the spare keys is unlocked?"

"Yeah." Levi swept back his long bangs. "It was unlocked when I got here this morning. I thought that was kind of weird."

"That settles it," Chuck said. "Barricade or not, we want the spare key to our room."

"So do I," Dorothy proclaimed and everyone in the room agreed with her.

"That's okay by me." Levi walked to the front desk and soon returned with a handful of keys, each one labeled with a room number.

Sarah took the keys for the twins' room and her room, placing them in her pocket. "Why didn't you mention the unlocked drawer before now?"

Levi's hair fell down his forehead again, making it difficult for Sarah to see his eyes. "I guess it just slipped my mind with everything going on."

"Is there anything else you've forgotten to mention?" Sarah asked, trying to keep her voice calm and even.

Levi thought for a moment and shook his head. "I don't think so."

"So Patrick gave you a key to the inn," she said slowly, "but not a master key to the drawer with the guest room keys. Is that right?"

Levi looked at her through his dark hair, "I guess so."

"And you're Patrick's only employee?"

"Yeah," Levi held another key out. "Do you still want the key to Patrick's room?" he asked and then handed it to her.

Sarah nodded and backed up a step so Levi could give the other guests their spare room keys.

Soon there were two keys left in Levi's palm, both to the empty room with the leaky shower.

"Well, I guess I know where I'll be sleeping tonight," he said, slipping them into the pocket of his denim jeans. Then he turned his attention back to the library shelves.

"Let's go, girls," Sarah said to the twins, waiting for another objection. But Vonnie didn't say a word as Amy and Audrey followed Sarah across the foyer to the back of the house.

They stopped in front of Patrick's door and Sarah started to insert the key in the brass lock when she noticed something odd. Bending down, Sarah examined the keyhole, finding the brass surface scratched and the keyhole edges bent and curled.

"What's wrong, Grandma?" Amy asked as she moved closer to the door.

Sarah carefully fingered the jagged edge. "It looks like someone tried to pry open the lock."

Someone who didn't know about the unlocked drawer of keys.

She pushed on the door and it swung open, the broken lock offering no resistance at all. Inside, it looked as if another blizzard had hit, only instead of snow, the room was blanketed with clothes and papers and overturned desk drawers.

"Wow," Audrey said as she followed Sarah into the room. "It didn't look like this before."

"No, it certainly didn't," Sarah murmured, realizing that all the guests had left the parlor at least once today, so she couldn't even narrow down her list of suspects.

Whoever had done this was looking for something and had been desperate enough to break into Patrick's room to find it. They'd obviously used a tool of some kind on the lock, a screwdriver or a knife.

Amy turned in a slow circle, taking in the whole room. "Who did this?"

"I don't know," Sarah replied.

The problem was that only part of the foyer and the front desk were visible from the parlor. Anyone could go to Patrick's room or the kitchen or upstairs without being detected as long as they were quiet about it. All of them had had more than enough time to search Patrick's room.

"It might be anybody," Sarah said. "We need evidence to know for sure." She pushed up the sleeves of her sweater. "So let's start digging and see what we can find."

Sarah walked over to the nightstand, looking at the three drawers that had been pulled out, their contents spilled all over the floor. She saw assorted coins and buttons, along with scraps of notepaper and several dog-eared paperbacks by a popular adventure novelist.

"What can I do to help?" Amy asked.

Sarah looked around the room. "Why don't you two start gathering up all these clothes for me and lay them out on the bed?"

Her gaze moved to the bed and she noticed the top mattress lay askew, as if someone had checked underneath it. The sheets had been pulled out and there was something odd about the pillows.

Amy's face fell. "That's it?"

"You can check all the pockets too," Sarah picked up one of the bed pillows and turned it over. A long, neat slit cut right through the pillowcase and the pillow itself. Fortunately, the pillow was made of foam instead of feathers or the room would be an even bigger mess than it was now. She checked the other pillow; it had been cut open too. At least now she knew whatever the culprit had been looking for could fit inside a pillow.

The girls began picking up the clothes and going through the pockets while Sarah started reading the scraps of paper on the floor. Most of them looked like simple reminders Patrick had made for himself. Repair window in library. Fix kitchen faucet. Buy eggs. However, there was one that caught her attention.

"Levi PO" next to a Hartford phone number.

She recognized the Hartford area code since it was the same one she had dialed when she had made reservations at the inn. But what did PO mean? Levi had said his last name was Prince, so the upper case O didn't fit.

She was still pondering the note when she heard a squeal of delight.

"Look what I found!" Audrey dug a key out of a blue shirt pocket and held it triumphantly in the air. "Maybe it's the key to the cellar!"

"That's wonderful, Audrey." Sarah walked over to look at it. "Good job."

Amy turned around and picked up another pile of clothes on the floor and threw them onto the bed. A shoe flew out of the pile and hit Audrey's shoulder.

"Hey, watch out," Audrey cried, reaching up to rub her shoulder. "That hurt."

Amy rolled her eyes. "Oh it did not. Don't be such a baby."

Audrey bent down and picked up the shoe. "Then let's see how you like it."

Sarah stepped between them. "Audrey, please put the shoe down. I didn't come in here to watch you girls fight."

"Yeah," Amy told her sister.

Audrey flashed a gloating smile. "Well, at least I found something." She held up the key. "Here, Grandma."

Sarah took it from her. "I'm afraid it's not the key to the padlock though. This is a skeleton key and quite an old one by the looks of it."

"Ha," Amy said.

"That's enough," Sarah said. "And you need to apologize to your sister for hitting her with that shoe. I know it was an accident, but she still got hurt."

"Why do you always take her side?" Amy said.

"I'm not taking any sides," Sarah said gently. "I want us to work together. I need all the help I can get to solve this mystery."

Amy's gaze dropped to the bed. "Sorry," she mumbled.

"It's okay," Audrey told her. "It really didn't hurt that much." Then she turned to Sarah. "You don't think this is the key to the cellar?"

"It's too old for that padlock," Sarah replied. "It's probably a key to a vintage dresser drawer or a rolltop desk. Lots of the old antiques here have simple locks that a skeleton key can open." She looked around the room for such a lock, but all of Patrick's furniture was too modern and none of the drawers had locks. She slipped the key into her pocket and moved on to his dresser while the girls continued sorting through his clothes. First, she replaced all the dresser drawers just to make it easier to search through the mess on the floor.

There were several bills scattered about, many of them past due.

She picked up one from the pile with Hartford Wireless Services stamped at the top. The amount due was four figures and there was a message typed in red at the bottom of the bill: Due to nonpayment of this bill we are discontinuing your wireless service and sending your delinquent account to our collection agency.

So the jovial innkeeper who had greeted them Friday evening had money problems. He certainly hadn't acted like it. Perhaps that had all been a show—or a reason for spiking his cola.

But these bills didn't explain the blood on the parlor floor or Patrick's disappearance. No, something had definitely happened here. Patrick's money problems might play a part in it, but they weren't the sole reason. They certainly weren't the reason someone had broken into his room and made such a big mess.

Sarah sorted through the rest of the bills—water, electric, gas, and cable. All unpaid. She put them aside and picked up a handful of travel brochures to the Caribbean. Many people longed for a tropical vacation in the middle of winter, but Patrick didn't have enough money to pay his bills much less plan a cruise or a trip to the Bahamas. Must just be good daydreaming material.

"How's it going, girls?" Sarah asked, placing the brochures next to the bills.

"It's kind of boring," Audrey admitted, tossing a T-shirt aside.

"We're going to find something," Amy said, digging through the pockets of a suit coat. "I just know it."

After Sarah was done fishing through the items on the floor, she walked into the bathroom and checked all the drawers and cupboards. The bathroom was in better shape than the bedroom and sitting area, but someone had still searched it. The door to the medicine cabinet was hanging open and several of the items on the shelves were in disarray. Even the top of the toilet tank had been removed and set to one side. She looked inside but didn't see anything unusual.

The culprit had been thorough in his search, but there was a sense of frustration in the way things had been tossed about. Sarah returned to the main room and found the girls sitting on the bed. "Done?"

"We checked every pocket," Amy replied. "And all we found was that stupid key."

Audrey stood up. "Can we go back to the parlor now?"

"I'm just about ready." Sarah took another look around, wondering if she'd missed anything. Then she saw Patrick's wallet still on top of the dresser, exactly where it had been when they'd all checked the room that morning. She picked it up and looked inside.

The cash and credit cards were still there, along with Patrick's driver's license. She took them all out and placed them on the dresser. Then she noticed something under the leather flap that kept the dollar bills in place. She lifted the flap and saw a small, black-and-white photograph of a newborn baby swaddled in a cotton blanket.

The edges of the photo were brown with age, the paper wrinkled. She couldn't tell from the picture whether the baby was a boy or a girl. She turned it over, but there was nothing written on the back.

No name. No date. Nothing.

Audrey stepped up beside her. "Oh look at the baby! It's so little."

Along with the delinquent bills, the skeleton key, and the ten gallons of gasoline in the shed, it was another clue about the missing man, one she'd add to the growing list.

Sarah still had no idea what had happened to Patrick, and she couldn't make any sense of the clues she had. Somehow she had to find a missing link or two that tied all these clues together.

Before it was too late for Patrick Maguire.

CHAPTER NINE

Bella was the only one who noticed Sarah and the girls return to the parlor. She sat in her infant seat on the floor, smiling and kicking her legs in the air when she saw Audrey appear in the doorway.

The rest of the group sat at the game table playing Scrabble, which they'd found in the library along with an assortment of other board games. Sarah sat down on the settee, her notebook in hand, while Amy headed to the library and Audrey sat on the floor to play with Bella.

Sarah started cataloguing the items she'd found in Patrick's room.

- Broken door lock
- Skeleton key
- Delinquent bills
- Phone number with Levi's name and the letters PO
- Sliced pillows
- Travel brochures
- Unidentified baby picture

As she wrote, she could feel the skeleton key in her pocket and planned to try it out whenever she came across a locked drawer just to see what she might find inside.

"I think we need to set a time limit." Finn leaned back in his chair and tilted his face toward the ceiling.

Those were the first words spoken since Sarah and the girls had returned to the parlor. The Scrabble players sat around the table rearranging the letter tiles in the racks in front of them.

"Look outside," Chuck said, one hand hovering over his rack. "None of us is leaving here anytime soon."

Sarah's gaze moved to the window, half covered with snow. The feeling of being buried alive washed over her and she closed her eyes and prayed for peace of mind and heart. They would find Patrick. They would get out of here. They would be all right.

She opened her eyes in time to see Chuck place a word on the board. "That's nine points for me."

Dorothy arched a brow. "Now you've left the triple word score wide open for Finn and he's already way ahead. That's not very good strategy."

"I know what I'm doing," Chuck said.

Dorothy shook her head as Finn connected a couple of tiles to the word Chuck had just laid down.

"Seven points plus the triple word score makes it twenty-one points for me," Finn said. "Thanks, Chuck."

Chuck sank down in his chair.

"*Dah*?" Levi pointed to Finn's word on the Scrabble board. "That's not a real word."

"Is that a challenge?" Finn asked him. "You'll lose your turn if you're wrong, you know."

"Yes, it's a challenge." Levi reached for the dictionary beside him. "And I'm not wrong."

"I want someone else to look up the word," Finn told him.

"Why?" Levi looked up from the dictionary. "You're not accusing me of cheating, are you?"

"Some people can't help cheating." An odd smile tipped up the corner of Finn's mouth. "It's in their blood."

Levi froze. "What's that supposed to mean?"

"I think we both know what it means."

Levi slowly stood up, a muscle twitching in his jaw. He didn't say anything for three long beats. Then he dropped the dictionary on the table in front of Dorothy. "Everything is a game to you, isn't it, Hawkins? Too bad you always come out a loser."

Finn stared at him, then got up from the table and walked toward him.

For a long moment, no one said anything. The only sound in the room was the crackle and hiss of the fire.

"Chuck," Vonnie murmured, elbowing her husband in the ribs, "do something."

Chuck cleared his throat. "C'mon guys, it's just a game."

"That's right." Finn stopped only a few inches away from Levi. "I guess you're even better at games than I am."

The two men stared at each for a long, tense moment, until Dorothy broke the silence.

"*Dah* is a real word," Dorothy said, the dictionary open in front of her. "It means a dash used in radio or telegraph code."

Finn smiled at Levi. "Who's the loser now?"

Levi turned around and stalked out of the room without saying a word.

The game had produced more questions than answers. And more riddles to solve. The other players returned to their game while Finn walked over to an empty chair by a window and sat down to read the newspaper. Sarah joined him there, leaning against the windowsill.

"You certainly know how to push Levi's buttons."

Finn lowered the newspaper. "He's a kid. Anyone could push his buttons."

"But you're a lot smarter than just anyone. So why push?"

Finn suddenly looked thoughtful. "Entertainment, I guess. I'm bored out of my mind. I hate being cooped up like this. Needling Levi gives me something to do."

Sarah believed it was an honest answer, even if it wasn't very flattering. "What brought you to the Red Clover Inn?"

"A business acquaintance recommended it." He stared out at the falling snow. "I'll have to remember to thank him."

Sarah noticed the newspaper was open to the classified section. "You never told me what you do for a living."

"No, I didn't."

She hoped he wasn't going to start playing his little games with her. "So what do you do?"

"I'm in real estate."

"You sell houses?"

"Commercial real estate," he clarified, turning to the next page. "The market's been a little down lately, so I'm exploring other options."

"Is that what brought you to Hartford?"

"Yes."

She was close enough to see a sheen of sweat form on his dark brow. For some reason, her questions were making him very nervous.

Sarah noticed the purplish blue hue of his black eye spreading along his cheekbone. "I hate to say it, but your black eye looks even worse than it did this morning. How did it happen again?"

He lowered the newspaper far enough for her to see the anger burning in his eyes. "Why don't you ask me what you really want to know? Did I hurt Patrick? The answer is no."

He lifted the newspaper again, shielding his face from her. "Now please leave me alone, Sarah."

An hour later, everyone sat at the dining room table to eat the dinner Vonnie had prepared. They'd eaten such a late breakfast that they'd skipped lunch altogether, just sneaking some tea or a leftover roll if they felt hungry.

"I hope everyone likes tuna salad sandwiches," Vonnie said, setting the platter on the table. Then she looked over at Sarah. "Did you say there were some potato chips in the pantry?"

"I'll get them," Sarah offered, rising from the table and heading for the kitchen.

But when she entered the pantry, the potato chips weren't on the shelf where she'd seen them before. "What in the world?" Sarah muttered to herself as she searched the other shelves. She looked again, certain she must have missed them. Then she returned to the dining room.

"The chips are gone."

"Maybe Chuck ate them," Finn said, taking a tuna sandwich from the platter.

"I certainly did not," Chuck replied.

"I saw them this morning when we were trying to figure out how to get into the cellar. I know it's not a big deal, but it's still a little strange," said Sarah.

Everyone looked around the table at each other, but no one confessed to taking the potato chips.

"I don't even like potato chips," Natalie said.

Chuck looked over at Finn. "Maybe you took them out to the porch with you during your smoke."

Finn laughed. "No, but it's a bag of potato chips, people. What's the big deal?"

Vonnie sniffed. "Well, it makes it hard to plan a meal, that's all."

Sarah found it odd that no one would admit to taking the chips. "Finn's right. It's certainly not a crime to eat a bag of chips. We all have free run of the kitchen."

Levi whispered something to Natalie, who was seated beside him, but Sarah couldn't make out the words. He even held Bella for a short while so Natalie could eat her tuna sandwich in peace.

Sarah barely touched her food, still unable to eat much while Patrick was missing. Instead, she studied the people around her, intently listening for any clues that might point her to the guilty party.

After supper, Sarah cleared the table while Vonnie pulled her peach cobbler out of the oven. A wonderful, sweet aroma filled the air as she set the dish on the stove top.

"That looks delicious." Sarah put a stack of dirty dishes on the counter and walked over for a closer look. Golden syrup bubbled around the peaches and the cobbler dough had just the right crispness.

"It's my mom's recipe and it tastes even better than it looks," Vonnie said proudly. She pulled open the drawer next to the stove and pulled out a serving spoon. "Can you get those dessert plates out of the cupboard and bring them over here? I want to serve this while it's still warm."

"Of course." Sarah realized this was the perfect opportunity to talk to Vonnie. Usually she and Chuck were stuck together like glue. "This place is so homey, isn't it? I knew I wanted to stay here as soon as I heard about it. Do you come here often?"

"Oh my, no." Vonnie began dishing up generous portions of cobbler. "We just happened upon it on our way back from visiting Mom in New Jersey. That's where she grew up. She lives in a nursing facility in her hometown and we don't get a chance to go there as often as we'd like."

"I'm lucky my father lives in a nursing home right in town. He's ninety-seven."

"About the same age as my mother." Vonnie filled the last dessert plate and licked her finger. "She's got dementia though, so she doesn't usually know us when we visit anymore."

Sarah's heart went out to her. "My dad's memory comes and goes. He's generally in good spirits, though, which is a blessing."

"So is Mom. She likes to sing to me when we're there."

"She sounds lovely."

"She is. Chuck thinks we should move her to a nursing facility closer to Providence, but I don't want to take her away from her old friends and all the Remmer cousins. Some of them are residents there, even though she doesn't always remember them."

Sarah knew those connections could be especially important to people suffering from dementia.

Vonnie surveyed the dessert plates. "This cobbler tastes even better with whipped cream or ice cream. Do you suppose we have any?"

"I'll check."

"We were planning to leave for home today," Vonnie said. "All this snow sure wasn't in our travel plans."

"Do you both have jobs to get back to?" Sarah asked as she opened the freezer.

"Oh no. We're both retired. But it seems we're busier now than ever."

"I know what you mean." Sarah pulled a tub of vanilla ice cream out of the freezer. "Looks like we're in luck. Now we just have to find an ice cream scoop."

At Dorothy's suggestion, they all decided to take their dessert into the parlor and eat in front of the fireplace. The house was growing colder as night fell and the wind began to howl again outside.

"The last thing we need is more wind," Chuck said. "It will just blow the drifts higher."

"I'm starting to feel like we're never going to get out of here," Dorothy said.

Levi's fork scraped across his plate to catch the last few cobbler crumbs. "As long as we can eat like this...is there any left?"

"There sure is," Vonnie said. "It's in the kitchen. Help yourself."

As Levi headed for seconds, Chuck called out, "Just bring the pan back with you." Then he set his empty plate on the table beside him and rose to his feet.

"Where are you going?" Vonnie asked.

He pointed to the library. "I thought I'd try to find a book to take to bed with me tonight."

Sarah thought that was a good idea and headed for the library herself.

"What kind of books do you like to read?" Sarah asked as the two of them scanned the shelves.

"Oh pretty much anything really, as long as it has a good plot."

"Well, your room reminds me of a tropical island, with the bamboo fan and that Island Path quilt on your bed. Maybe you should try Robinson Crusoe."

He shook his head. "I prefer a lighter read."

He tilted his head back, his gaze fixed on the spot where the top shelf met the ceiling. "How are we supposed to reach the books way up there?"

"There's a ladder," she said, pointing out the rolling ladder on the other side of the room. "Although I'm not sure I want to climb that high."

He chuckled. "I know my knee doesn't. I've got to baby it or it gives out on me."

"Have you hurt it recently?"

He kept his gaze on the books. "It was a little stiff when I woke up this morning. That happens sometimes—especially in bad weather."

She lowered her voice so only he could hear her. "I thought you might have hurt it last night."

Chuck slowly turned around to face her. "What do you mean?"

She sensed he wanted to deny the scuffle with Patrick, but wasn't sure what she knew. "I had to go out to my car last night," she whispered. "It was late but I heard voices in the parlor."

Then she waited. Silence was an effective way to get people to open up. It made people uncomfortable and they often talked just to fill the void.

"It's not what you think," he said at last.

She waited, still not saying anything.

He took a step closer to her, lowering his voice another notch. "Look, it wasn't a real fight. Nobody threw a punch or anything."

"I'm sure you wouldn't hurt Patrick on purpose."

"Of course not. He fell right on top of me." Chuck sucked in a deep breath. "I had good reason to be upset. Vonnie and I made reservations months ago. She'd read all about this place and was so excited to celebrate our wedding anniversary here. But when we arrived we found out Patrick had given the room we wanted to someone else. Then he stuck us in that tropical nightmare.

"I admit I lost my temper," Chuck whispered, "and I felt sorry about it afterward. I was going to apologize to Patrick this morning, only...."

Sarah watched his face, knowing he wasn't a good game player. He looked sincere, but she couldn't be certain. He might be telling her part of the truth but not all of it. Chuck was holding something back.

Vonnie appeared in the doorway. "What's going on?"

"Nothing," he said, hastily pulling a random book off the shelf. "Just finishing up in here. I want some more of Paulette's peach cobbler before it's all gone."

"Then you'd better hurry. We're all getting ready to head upstairs soon," Vonnie said, her gaze moving between her husband and Sarah. "We've all had a long day."

Sarah walked over to the shelf with the Agatha Christie novels neatly arranged in a row. She selected *The Body in the Library,* one of her favorites.

If only Miss Marple were here to help her now, maybe she could explain why Vonnie and Chuck had just told her two completely different stories.

# CHAPTER TEN

Sarah stifled a yawn as she walked into her room. The girls came in behind her and headed straight for the connecting door. She smiled to herself, noting that they were too tired to even ask about staying up late tonight.

She was tired too.

So much had happened since she'd awakened to Dorothy's scream early this morning. Now, as she stood alone in her room, the mournful moan of the wind against the shingles made her shiver.

Sarah noticed a blinking light from her cell phone on the dresser. She had set her cell phone there when she and the girls had come upstairs earlier and had forgotten to take it downstairs with her.

Picking up the phone, she found another text message waiting for her. It was from Martha, but the message was just as vague and unsettling as before.

Must call me!

"Oh Martha," she groaned aloud. "What are you talking about?"

She knew the reason Martha kept her text messages so short was because it took her so long to type anything on her tiny cell phone keyboard. Sarah preferred face-to-face conversations too, or at least hearing a voice on the phone. But, thanks to her granddaughters, she had gotten used to receiving text messages and found them handy at times.

This was not one of those times.

Must call me!

Sarah looked at the message again and told herself that if it was a real emergency, Martha would take the time to send a longer text or keep calling until the call went through. That reassured her a little, but she knew it could still be something serious. And with the spotty cell reception, maybe Martha *was* repeatedly trying to call.

Sarah dialed Martha's number, hoping the call would go through this time. It rang once and stopped. She tried calling Jason's number but this time it didn't even ring before disconnecting.

Frustrated, Sarah tried sending a text message of her own. Her thumbs didn't fly over the keypad like Amy's and Audrey's on their phones, but she was able to punch out a short message to Martha. *What's wrong?*

She hit the send button, hoping Martha would see it right away and let her know what was happening. Setting the phone back on the dresser, Sarah picked up the remote control and turned on the television, trying to find something to distract herself so she wouldn't worry.

She tuned to the local news just in time for the weather report.

"More snow expected tomorrow, but this slow-moving storm system should be out of our area by Sunday night."

Sunday night. That meant that she most likely had until Monday morning to find the guilty party. She knew after the roads were cleared, everyone would scatter and it would be that much harder for the police to make an arrest. That gave them only thirty-six hours to find out what had happened to Patrick.

"The wind chill is going to get dangerously low for the rest of the weekend, so keep yourself and your pets indoors."

The anchorman thanked the meteorologist and turned to face the camera. "In other news, we have a report of one man taken to an area hospital with severe burns to his hands after he set fire to his own home. The police say his house was going into foreclosure and he wanted to collect the insurance money—"

Sarah switched off the television set, remembering all those gasoline cans in the shed and the travel brochures she'd found in Patrick's room.

Sarah sat down with her notebook and added all the new information she'd collected.

Chuck had admitted to fighting with Patrick. He had also lied to her about his reasons for coming here—or Vonnie had.

Levi hadn't bothered to mention the unlocked drawer.

Natalie claimed Bella was colicky, but the baby hadn't fussed the entire day.

Dorothy was quick to mention her arthritis though it didn't seem to hamper her knitting at all.

The few minutes it had taken Sarah to check into the inn on Friday evening had been long enough to discern that Levi and Patrick didn't have the best working relationship either. Levi also had the most knowledge about the inn and would know where to hide something. Or someone.

Her head was spinning and she hoped a good night's sleep would help her clear it. The one thing she knew for certain was that no one had been ruled out yet.

And she couldn't forget about Patrick or just assume he was innocent in all of this. He was an integral part of this puzzle, even if he was the missing piece.

A beep sounded from her cell phone and Sarah jumped up to get it. She pressed the text message button, but saw only the message she had tried to send with a big red X by it, indicating it hadn't gone through.

A creak sounded on the ceiling directly above her. Sarah stilled, her breath catching in her throat. Another creak followed and then a third. Those creaks didn't sound like an old house settling—they sounded distinctly like footsteps.

She stood rooted to the spot, her ears perked for more creaking sounds above her. A sudden rapping against the windowpane made her jump. Her heart raced as she walked over to the window and lifted the lace curtain. Bare tree branches flew toward her in the wind, knocking against the glass.

Dropping the curtain, Sarah took a deep breath, trying to steady herself. She walked over to the dresser and retrieved Maeve Maguire's Bible from the drawer and opened it to the first chapter in Joshua. Reading verse nine always comforted her in times like this.

"Have I not commanded you?" she read aloud. "Be strong and courageous. Do not be terrified; do not be discouraged, for the Lord your God will be with you wherever you go."

Sarah closed her eyes, taking the words to heart. The Lord your God will be with you wherever you go.

There wasn't a wind chill or a blizzard or a creaky house worth being afraid of. She needed to remember that when those troublesome emotions of worry and fear started to erode her sense of well-being.

Another creak sounded above her and a moment later the connecting door flew open, startling Sarah out of her peaceful reflection. "What on earth?"

Audrey ran inside, her blue eyes wide with fear. "Grandma, did you hear that?"

"You mean the creaking noises?"

Audrey nodded, wrapping her arms around herself. "I don't like it."

"I know, dear. Come here," Sarah said, pulling her close. The poor girl was breathing unevenly. "But there's no reason to be afraid. All old houses make noises like that. I'm sure your house does too."

"I know," she said. "But I'm used to those noises. These are just ... weird."

"I know."

"I still wish they would stop."

Sarah looked toward the connecting door. "What is Amy doing?"

"She called me a baby and went to take a shower." Audrey shivered. "Maybe I *am* a baby, but I don't like being alone in this place."

Sarah squeezed her tight. "You're not alone. I'm right here and God is with us too."

"Well, I sure wish he'd make all of these scary noises stop."

Sarah smiled. "Maybe he will. In the meantime, why don't you climb into my bed and—"

"Will you finish the story about Jenna and my dad?" Audrey interjected as she scrambled onto the bed and buried herself beneath the covers.

"I will." Sarah tucked the quilt around Audrey's shoulders. "Now where did we leave off?"

"Aunt Jenna used to hide from my dad all the time," Audrey said, "then something happened to make her promise never to hide again."

"Oh, that's right."

"So what happened?"

"Well, I'd better start at the beginning. You see, Grandpa Gerry always used to take your dad and Jenna on a big camping trip every summer. It was just the three of them.

The kids always looked forward to it and they were gone for a whole week."

"Didn't you miss them?"

"Of course I did, but sometimes mothers need a vacation too. Plus the kids got to spend some special time with their dad."

Audrey snuggled deeper into the bed. "Did they sleep in a tent?"

"They sure did. Grandpa Gerry believed in roughing it all the way. They ate the fish they caught and gathered mushrooms and berries."

She giggled into the pillow. "I can't picture my dad looking for berries."

"Your dad always made it a contest to see who could find the most. That made Jenna mad, too, because he raced around gathering berries when she just wanted to take her time and taste a few along the way."

Sarah paused in her storytelling. It was so easy to picture Gerry sitting at the kitchen table as he shared their camping escapades with her over a cup of coffee. Those happy days had flown by so quickly.

"What happened next, Grandma?"

"Well, most of the time, Grandpa Gerry took the kids camping on Mount Greylock, but this particular summer, he decided to try a different mountain. And now that the kids were older, he told them they were really going to live off the land. They had to make their own fishing poles when they got there and find all their own food."

Audrey yawned. "He didn't take any food along?"

"Well," Sarah said with a smile, "I think he put some food in the trunk, just in case the fishing didn't go well, but the kids didn't know about it. When they got there, they explored the area around their camping spot and Gerry set up some orange flags around it so the kids could find their way back if they got lost."

"That was smart," Audrey murmured, her eyelids looking heavy.

"Your grandpa was a smart man. After he set up the flags, Grandpa Gerry helped the kids make their fishing poles and sent them off together to catch supper in the nearby river while he put up the tent."

Sarah tenderly brushed a strand of blonde hair off Audrey's cheek. "On the way to the creek, your dad told Jenna that they were going to make a game of it to see who could catch the most fish and the loser would have to clean all of them. Jenna had always caught more fish than your father, so she practically ran to the river—" A soft snore made Sarah look down at Audrey. She was fast asleep, her hands tucked under her head. Sarah carefully rose from the bed, not wanting the movement to wake her. Then she put Maeve's Bible back in the drawer and began to tidy up the room before going to sleep herself.

The connecting door opened and Amy walked inside. She wore a T-shirt and sweatpants, her blonde hair woven into two wet braids. Her gaze went to the bed. "What's going on?"

"Your sister just fell asleep." She pulled her nightgown out of a drawer. "I think I'm going to leave her there for the night if you don't mind. She hasn't been feeling well today and I think a good night's sleep will help her feel better."

When Amy didn't say anything, Sarah looked over at her. "Will you be scared to sleep by yourself?"

"I'm not scared of anything." Amy walked over to the dresser and picked up Sarah's notebook. "Can I help with the case?"

"Well," Sarah started. "You can keep your eyes and ears open and report anything unusual."

Amy held up the notebook. "Maybe I should read all your notes tonight so I know what to look for."

Sarah gently took the notebook out of her hand. "I think it's a little late for that tonight. We can sit down after breakfast and read through everything together, okay? I want you to get a good night's sleep."

"But, Grandma—" Amy started, but stopped when she saw Sarah's no-nonsense face. "Okay. Good night."

Sarah ran a comb through her hair. "I'll be in soon to tuck you in."

Amy stood there for a moment and then turned around and walked through the connecting door.

Sarah removed her shoes and socks and changed into her flannel nightgown. The wood floor felt cold on her bare feet. She was just about to reach for her slippers when a loud crash sounded right outside the door.

Audrey's head popped up from the pillow. "What was that?"

"I don't know." Sarah hurried over to the door as Amy rushed inside.

"What's going on?"

"Stand back, Amy," Sarah said, unlocking the door and opening it a crack so she could see into the hallway. One of the brass chandeliers lay in pieces on the floor in front of her, the shards of glass sparkling under the light of the remaining chandeliers.

She opened the door a little farther when she saw the Thayers and Dorothy emerge from their rooms.

"What in the world happened out here?" Chuck asked, looking at Sarah.

"I don't know," she stepped into the hallway, motioning for Audrey and Amy to stay in the doorway.

Natalie carried Bella down the hallway, her eyes heavy with sleep. Finn and Levi soon joined them, forming a circle around the shattered chandelier.

"Everyone be careful of the broken glass," she warned and looked up at the plank ceiling, noticing the rotting wood where the chandelier had been. White paint had concealed the moisture underneath. "Looks like it was an accident."

"Are you sure about that?" Dorothy asked. "I thought I heard footsteps above me just a short while ago. I think someone was up in the attic."

"I heard them too," Finn said. "I blamed the wind at the time, but now—"

"Everybody, just chill," Levi said. "The roof leaks, okay? Snow seeps into the attic and melts on the floor. I've told Patrick we need to have the roof fixed, but he always puts it off—"

Suddenly the lights went out and they were lost in a sheet of blackness.

"Grandma?" Audrey called out. "Amy, where are you?"

"I'm right here," Sarah shouted back. "But don't move. The glass will cut your feet."

"Chuck," Vonnie screamed. "I can't see you. What's happening?"

Natalie cried out as Bella began to sob in her arms. "I can't see anything."

"Nobody move," Sarah shouted again, hearing the panic in their voices. "There's broken glass everywhere."

"Somebody must have planned this," Dorothy said, her voice trembling. "We're trapped here in the dark, completely helpless."

Her voice faded as the sound of heavy footsteps moved toward them.

CHAPTER ELEVEN

As the footsteps came closer, Sarah glimpsed a yellow glow of light. The light grew stronger until she recognized Levi walking toward them carrying a rusty kerosene lantern.

The light illuminated his bare arm and she could see a crudely inked tattoo peeking out from beneath the sleeve of his green T-shirt.

She placed a hand on her chest, trying to calm her erratic heartbeat. "Levi, it's you."

Natalie stared at him. "But you were standing right here beside me when the lights went out."

"Yeah," Levi said. "I remembered seeing this lantern in my room and ran to get it as soon as the electricity went out. I figured we'd need it."

"How did you find your way in the dark?" Vonnie asked.

"I'm pretty familiar with this place, Mrs. Thayer," Levi said. "I can find my way around in the dark."

Vonnie wrung her hands together. "I still think someone cut the lights on purpose. I've been hearing strange noises ever since we went to bed."

"You sure it's not just the house settling?" Sarah asked. "I've been hearing noises too."

Vonnie shook her head. "No, they were coming from the ceiling and they definitely sounded like footsteps to me. I'm almost sure of it."

"I heard them too," Audrey cried.

"The circuit box is in the pantry behind the shelf of cereal boxes," Levi said, "so even if someone was in the attic they couldn't cut the lights."

"The sounds I heard were coming from outside my door," Natalie said in a low voice. Bella lay with her head on Natalie's shoulder, tears gleaming in her eyes. "I thought it was just the house settling or the wind or something, but now I'm not so sure."

Sarah wasn't sure now either, although her better judgment told her a creaking house was perfectly normal. However, that would make it the only normal thing that had happened here lately. Either they were all becoming paranoid or someone was trying to scare them.

And doing a great job of it.

"Well, I'm not going to stand around here all night listening to ghost stories," Finn said, carefully avoiding the broken glass as he headed for the stairs.

"Where are you going?" Chuck called after him.

"Down to the parlor." Finn reached for the polished banister rail, using it to guide him as he was swallowed up in the darkness. "The fireplace will provide a lot more light than that lantern."

Sarah helped the girls maneuver around the broken glass. "He's right. We'll need the fire to keep warm too. With the wind chill outside, this house is going to get very cold very fast."

By the time they all reached the parlor, Finn was stirring the glowing embers in the grate back to life and adding more wood on top of them. It didn't take long for a bright orange flame to curl around the fresh logs, casting light and warmth into the shadowy room.

Levi moved toward the foyer. "Now that the fire is lit, I'll take the lantern and go start up the generator. Then we'll have heat and lights again."

Chuck watched him leave before turning to the rest of the group. "At this point can't we all agree that only someone with intimate knowledge of this old building would be able to pull off making Patrick disappear like this?"

Sarah sat down on the settee with Amy and Audrey on either side of her. They snuggled up close, drawing their legs up under themselves for warmth.

Sarah looked over at Vonnie, who sat close to the fire, her slender arms wrapped around her waist. Only this afternoon, Vonnie had been making a case against Finn. Now her husband was blaming Levi.

"He had that lantern within seconds of the power outage," Chuck continued. "And he's the only one here who would know his way around in the dark."

Finn set the fireplace poker in the rack and brushed his hands together.

"Now that Patrick's gone," Chuck said, "Levi is in charge of the place. He might be looting it as we speak."

Natalie snorted. "Looting what?"

"Plenty of antiques, for one," Dorothy said. She stood by the window, her wrinkled skin looking paler than usual against the dark gold drapes.

"That's ridiculous," Natalie said. "Levi's done nothing but help everyone. While you're accusing him of something horrible, he's trudging out into the snow to start the generator. If he were guilty, he could just let us all freeze to death."

"If we freeze to death, so does Levi," Finn replied. "We're all stuck here together until the snow clears."

"That may be true," Dorothy admitted. Her petite frame was emphasized by her oversize white terry cloth robe and slippers. "But I think Natalie is right about the boy. He's gone above and beyond the call of duty. At this point, I see no reason to suspect him of foul play."

Sarah leaned toward the girls and whispered, "How are you doing?"

"Okay," Audrey said. "It's still too dark in here for me. And I'm cold."

"Baby," Amy muttered under her breath.

"I am not a baby!" Audrey hissed.

Sarah put her arms around both of them, pulling them closer to her. "We've got to all stick together, remember? That means not fighting with each other."

"Grandma, I—," Amy began, but before she could finish, a loud, clanging noise reverberated through the house.

Natalie whirled around to stare into the pitch-black foyer. "What in the world is that?"

Audrey gripped Sarah's hand so tightly Sarah couldn't feel her fingers. Amy emitted a small, frightened cry as the clanging continued. The way it echoed around them made it impossible for Sarah to determine where it was coming from.

"See, I told you it was Levi," Chuck said, turning to the group. "He's got to be making that noise. He's the only one who's not here."

"But why would he do such a thing?" Natalie asked, rhythmically rubbing Bella's back as if to soothe them both.

"I don't know," Chuck said.

The clanging suddenly stopped.

Nobody moved or spoke. Sarah's chest felt tight and she realized she was holding her breath. She released it and concentrated on taking slow, deep breaths. The girls were already teetering on the edge of panic. She needed to stay calm for them.

"Okay," Chuck said softly. "If Levi comes back in the next five minutes, then we'll know for sure it was him making that noise."

As soon as he said the words, the clanging started again. It was softer this time, making the tinny, echoing sound even more eerie. No one said anything for several long minutes as Sarah listened intently to the clangs, looking for any rhythm or pattern.

But as far as she could tell, there was no message in the clangs. They were disjointed and seemed completely random.

"This is really freaking me out," Natalie said, retreating toward the library. "What's going on here?"

"It couldn't be a…ghost, could it?" Audrey asked, her voice trembling.

"Oh for pity's sake," Dorothy said in exasperation. "This inn clanged the same way fifty years ago. It's just bad plumbing."

CHAPTER TWELVE

"Y" ou girls stay here," Sarah whispered. "I'll be right back."

Sarah left the settee and walked over to the window where Dorothy stood watching the storm. "It's quite a blizzard, isn't it?"

"One of the worst I've ever seen." Dorothy's wrinkled hand stretched over the cold windowpane.

Sarah leaned closer and lowered her voice. "How do you know this inn had bad plumbing fifty years ago?"

"You must have misunderstood me," she answered after a moment.

"I don't think so."

A smile played on Dorothy's lips. "I'm just an old woman, Sarah. I get confused easily. I must have been thinking of some other inn."

"You've never seemed confused to me," Sarah whispered. "Quite the opposite, actually."

"Well, thank you, dear. I'll take that as a compliment." Dorothy avoided her gaze. "I believe it is common knowledge that many old houses have bad plumbing. I've certainly heard that kind of clanking in other places before."

"But you weren't making a general statement," Sarah said. "You said the inn clanked like that fifty years ago."

"What difference does it make? I think you're nitpicking."

"What are you holding back, Dorothy?"

Dorothy smoothed her white hair with trembling fingers. "You make it sound as if I've purposely been deceiving everyone."

"If you're not, why do you look so guilty?"

Her green eyes dropped and she suddenly looked every day of her seventy-two years.

A tense silence stretched between them.

"All right," Dorothy whispered. "I *have* been to the Red Clover before." She sank into a wing chair, her face as pale as the snow. "My husband and I stayed here during our honeymoon fifty years ago. We had such a wonderful time that I wanted to relive the memories."

"Then why keep it a secret?"

"I wasn't trying to keep it a secret. Coming here without him is one of the most difficult things I've ever done—," Dorothy's voice cracked and she paused a moment before continuing. "I thought it would make me feel better to re-member how happy we were. The last time I stayed here, Leo and I had our whole lives ahead of us and now he's gone. It's harder than I thought. There have been times this weekend when I wasn't sure if I could hide the pain." She shook her head. "I don't know that I can make you understand."

Sarah knew the lonely void losing a spouse left in your life. Time and prayer, as well as friends and fam-ily, had helped to heal her pain. But Dorothy's was still so fresh—Sarah could see it etched in every line on her face.

"I do understand," Sarah said softly.

Dorothy brushed her hand across her mouth. "I should have been honest with all of you from the beginning. It was selfish of me to keep it to myself—especially considering what's happened."

"Did Patrick know?"

Dorothy nodded. "I pointed out the room Leo and I had stayed in during our honeymoon. He was sweet enough to give it to me."

Chuck's angry words about Patrick giving their room to someone else came back to Sarah—and there was something else that niggled in the back of her mind, but she couldn't quite put her finger on it. Perhaps it was the late hour. They were all tired and apprehensive about the loss of power and the strange noises in the night.

The color gradually returned to Dorothy's face and she looked steadier than she had a few moments ago. "I never should have come here. I thought this trip would bring back all the happy memories Leo and I shared together, but so far it's been a nightmare."

"It will be all right," Sarah said, feeling a little guilty for forcing her confession.

Tears shimmered in Dorothy's eyes, but she blinked them back. "I just want to go home."

Bella began to cry, as if sharing the sentiment. Audrey walked over to help Natalie with the baby while Amy sat on the settee not saying a word.

Sarah's gaze moved to Finn, who had also been unusually quiet during this whole ordeal. He stood by the fireplace, one hand braced against the mantle as he stared into the flames. He was somewhere very far away and the look in his eyes made her heart ache for him.

Sarah's gaze moved back to the window. Moonlight peeked through the clouds and reflected off the snow. A fine white powder of blowing snow shimmered in the light. She couldn't tell if the snow had finally stopped or was still falling.

A sudden homesickness tightened her throat. She missed her cozy house in Maple Hill. She missed talking with Martha and visiting her father at Bradford Manor. She missed Jason and Maggie and her friends at Bridge Street Church.

She missed Gerry.

Sarah turned away from the window before her emotions overcame her. A silly reaction, given that she'd only been away from home for two days. But the fact that they'd been cut off from communication with the outside world made it seem so much longer.

At least she had Amy and Audrey to keep her company, unlike Dorothy, who had to face this frightening situation alone. And Natalie, who had a baby to care for and protect.

Sarah had her faith too, and took this moment to silently thank God for all the blessings in her life. *Lord, you've given me so much—good friends and a loving family. I pray you wrap your loving arms around everyone here and give us all the strength to face whatever lies ahead.*

The electricity suddenly came on, flooding the parlor with light.

"Hooray," Vonnie shouted, as others began to applaud.

Even Bella stopped fussing, her teary blue eyes staring at the glowing chandelier above her.

A few moments later, Levi returned to the parlor, his cheeks red from the cold. "As you can see, I got the generator going, but there's a problem."

Finn's face darkened. "Now what?"

"We have ten gallons of gasoline on hand and that's only enough for four, maybe five hours."

Sarah moved away from the window and joined the others. "You use gasoline to power the generator?"

Levi nodded. "Patrick always keeps a few gallons on hand in case of emergencies, but that generator is a gas-guzzler. Costs a fortune to run."

Finn turned to face him. "So you're saying we could run out?"

"If the power isn't restored soon," Levi replied, "yeah, we could be in trouble."

"But the generator will last through the night, right?" Chuck asked.

Levi hesitated. "It should. But we won't have any electricity in the morning. If we turn it off while we sleep—"

"No way," Vonnie interjected, crossing her arms in front of her. "It's not safe in this house and I refuse to be trapped here in the dark on top of everything else. I say we leave the generator on."

Finn snorted. "So you're going to run us out of fuel because you're scared of the dark?"

Chuck stepped in front of his wife. "Now hold on there, Hawkins. You have no call to talk to my wife that way. She has a point."

"C'mon, Chuck," Finn said. "She's being silly. It makes sense for the house to be dark while we're sleeping. Why waste what little fuel we have when we don't need it?"

Sarah could see both points of view. The rational part of her knew they'd need the electricity tomorrow for cooking and warmth. But another part of her agreed with

Vonnie—there was something about the dark, creaking house that she found almost sinister.

"So what do you want to do?" Levi looked around the room. "Turn it off or leave it on?"

"I have an idea," Sarah said before Vonnie and Finn resumed their debate. "Why don't we leave the generator on long enough to gather some supplies, like candles, flashlights, and extra blankets. That way we won't be completely in the dark until morning."

Dorothy nodded. "Now that makes sense to me."

"Me too," Natalie said and looked over at Vonnie. "Will that work for you?"

"I suppose so," Vonnie said hesitantly. "But morning can't come soon enough for me."

"I'll start looking for flashlights and stuff," Levi said, heading back out of the parlor. "And someone better clean up that glass. There's a broom and dustpan in the hallway closet upstairs. There should be a handheld vacuum in there too."

Before Sarah could volunteer, the other guests disappeared, some heading for the stairs and others toward the kitchen.

Sarah led the girls upstairs and around the broken glass into her room. "You two stay in here while I clean this up. It shouldn't take too long."

The cleaning supplies were right where Levi had said, and a few minutes later, Sarah began sweeping up the glass.

Chuck sidled by her carrying an armful of blankets. "Do you mind? I'm trying to get through here."

Sarah moved out of the way, but he entered his room before she could reply. She swept the glass shards into the dustpan and disposed of them before using the battery-operated handheld vacuum to pick up the slivers of glass left in the carpet.

Vonnie suddenly appeared beside her. Sarah turned off the vacuum as the woman leaned in close.

"Did you notice that the clanging stopped when Levi came back upstairs? Vonnie whispered.

"It stopped before that, didn't it?" Sarah said.

"Well, we know for certain that none of the rest of us caused it. I'm just saying the clanging happened while Levi was out of sight."

Vonnie headed back to her room while Sarah stared after her. Then she finished vacuuming up the glass before returning the cleaning supplies to the closet.

When she walked back into her room, she saw the girls already preparing for the impending blackout. They had gathered the decorative candles from the dresser and nightstand and placed them in Amy's empty backpack.

"Do you have any candles in your room?" Sarah asked as she retrieved a book of matches from the top drawer of her nightstand.

Both girls shook their heads. "We have the bearskin rug, though," Amy offered. "I bet that could keep us warm."

Audrey wrinkled her nose. "I think I'd rather freeze to death than wake up with that thing staring me in the face."

"It's not real," Amy reminded her. "It's just like a doll."

"With fangs," Audrey murmured.

Sarah took another look around the room and moved toward the door. "I remember seeing some extra quilts and blankets in the attic. The sooner we gather the supplies we need, the sooner we can go back to bed."

The attic had only one light, a naked bulb screwed into a rafter in the center of the room. Dust tickled Sarah's nose as she walked through the attic door.

"It's kind of spooky up here at night," Amy said.

"Now who's being a baby?" Audrey said as they followed Sarah inside.

She ignored their bickering, intent on finding the blankets and leaving the attic as quickly as possible. She agreed with Amy—it was a little spooky up there. If the lights went out again, this wasn't where she wanted them to be.

"Where are the quilts?" Amy asked.

Sarah stopped and looked around. There were so many boxes and pieces of furniture crowding the attic she couldn't get her bearings. It had been much easier to see everything in the light of day.

"I see them!" Audrey cried out. She grabbed Sarah's arm and pulled her to a pile of tattered quilts stacked on an old sideboard.

"Good job," Sarah said as Amy trailed behind them.

Sarah picked up a century-old Victorian crazy quilt from the top of the stack and carefully unfolded it. Moth holes stood out like freckles in many of the vintage fabric pieces, revealing the white foundation fabric underneath. The red feather stitching was loose in several places as well.

Amy wrinkled her nose. "What stinks?"

Sarah held the quilt closer and inhaled. A musty odor invaded her nostrils. "It's the quilt."

"The rest of them smell too," Audrey said, waving a hand in front of her face. "Can we put them in the washing machine before we use them?"

Sarah shuddered at the suggestion. "Oh no. That would ruin them for sure."

Audrey shrugged. "They already look pretty ruined to me."

She was right. If they used these quilts most of them would fall apart. Sarah couldn't let that happen. These were pieces of history that should be restored and treasured. They'd have to find something else to keep them warm.

Sarah carefully folded the fragile quilt and set it back on top of the stack. Strong odors of mildew and a hint of something rusty or metallic emanated from the quilts and started to make her feel queasy. She quickly stepped away from them, seeking some fresh air.

"Can we go back downstairs now?" Audrey asked.

Sarah hesitated, not wanting to leave the attic empty-handed. "Let's look up here a little bit longer and see if there's anything else that might be useful."

As they wove through the maze of boxes and furniture, Sarah found herself wishing she'd made time to get the flashlight so she could see into the shadowy corners. She knew if they didn't find anything tonight, they could always return in the morning to look again.

She was about to give up when her gaze landed on a box from a regional chain store that specialized in housewares. Walking over to the box, she lifted the lid. "Blankets!"

"Really?" Amy peered into the box. "Wow, you're right. And these blankets aren't old and stinky."

In fact, they were brand-new. Sarah lifted out four thermal blankets, each one still wrapped in plastic, and handed two to Amy and two to Audrey. Then she moved the empty box aside to see if there were more boxes behind it.

Instead, she found something even more unusual. A small, antique chest, the silver tarnished almost beyond recognition. She moved closer to the light, unable to read the words engraved on the top of the box. She pulled a tissue from the pocket of her robe and rubbed it vigorously over the tarnished silver.

"What is that, Grandma?" Amy asked, peering over her shoulder.

"I don't know," Sarah said, surprised to find this small, unique antique in the attic. The chest was no bigger than a bread box and looked out of place amidst the larger pieces of furniture scattered around them.

As she rubbed the tarnish away, the words became visible.

"Maeve Ryan," Sarah said aloud.

"Who's Maeve Ryan?" Audrey asked.

"Patrick's grandmother." Sarah wondered why the chest hadn't been placed in her room along with the rest of Maeve's things. With a little polish, the silver chest would be quite lovely.

She tried to open the lid, but it was locked. Then she noticed the keyhole and mental gears clicked together. There had to be a reason Patrick kept this beautiful chest hidden in the attic. Just like there had to be a reason he carried the skeleton key that opened it in his shirt pocket.

"We have to go back to my room," Sarah announced, already heading for the attic door.

"What did you find?" Audrey asked as the girls hurried to keep up with her.

"I'm not sure, but if we're lucky, we'll soon figure it out."

When they reached the hallway, Sarah heard a door open. She grabbed a blanket from Audrey and placed it over the silver chest.

Natalie emerged from her room. "What's going on?"

"We found—" Amy began.

"Some blankets in the attic," Sarah interjected. "Do you need any extras?"

"No," Natalie said, looking between the three of them. "I'm good."

"Well, good night," Sarah said to her, then moved toward her door. When she glanced back she saw Natalie still standing in the hallway staring after them.

When they were inside Sarah's room, she retrieved the skeleton key that Audrey had found. She inserted it into the lock of the antique chest and twisted it, waiting for the silver lid to pop open.

Only it didn't pop.

Audrey's mouth drooped. "It doesn't work?"

Sarah wasn't ready to give up that easily. She jiggled the key, aware an old lock could be rusty and difficult to open. At last, she felt something give in the lock mechanism and she was able to turn the key far enough for the lid to ease open.

"You did it!" Audrey squealed.

Sarah opened the lid, eager to see what she'd find inside. There was a deed to the inn and some loan papers. Patrick obviously used this chest as a lockbox for his important papers. She set the documents aside and dug further, hoping to find something that could help her solve this case. But all she saw was the back of a small, flattened box.

Sarah lifted it out of the chest, feeling something hard and flat through the cardboard. Then she turned the box over and saw the label. "Sentinel."

"Sentinel," Amy echoed. "Why does that sound familiar?"

"Because it's the same brand name as the padlock on the cellar door." Sarah opened the box and saw something that could break the case wide open. "I think we just found the key to the cellar."

CHAPTER THIRTEEN

S arah had to think.

She and the twins could search the cellar alone or she could tell the rest of the group about the key she had found. While there might be an advantage to seeing the cellar before anyone else, Sarah couldn't be certain it was safe. Despite Levi's assurances that the clanging noise they'd all heard was due to bad plumbing, they didn't know what—or who—might be down there.

Besides, she wanted to observe everyone's reaction when she broke the news about finding the cellar key. That might tell her more than exploring the cellar itself.

Her decision made, Sarah and the girls returned to the parlor. Natalie was rocking her baby while the other guests sat around the game table playing a board game.

"Can everyone gather around, please?" Sarah said, then waited for them to join her near the fireplace.

"I think I've found something." Sarah held up the key, watching closely for their reactions. "It's the key to the cellar."

Levi walked over to examine it. "Where did you find it?"

"I came across it in the attic," Sarah said, "while I was looking for blankets. I recognized the brand name as the same one on the padlock."

"Who cares where she found it," Finn said, moving toward the doorway. "Let's find out what's down there."

Everyone sprang up and followed Finn. Sarah prayed every step of the way that they'd find Patrick in the cellar alive.

She observed the others as they made their way to the pantry. Levi led the way, his long stride quickly diminishing the distance between him and the cellar door. Finn was right behind him, grim determination etched on his face. Natalie followed with the baby, her mouth tight. Dorothy moved with a steady pace, trying to keep up. She braced one hand against the wall every few steps as if to steady herself. She was followed by the Thayers, who were whispering to each other.

Sarah picked up the pace as she and the twins brought up the rear, hoping to overhear what Chuck and Vonnie were saying. She figured whoever had the original cellar key never expected anyone to find the copy.

When they reached the pantry, everyone stood aside while Sarah made her way to the cellar door. She inserted the key into the padlock and held her breath, wondering if she had brought all of them here for nothing.

She turned the key and the padlock snapped open.

"It worked," Dorothy said.

Sarah removed the padlock from the door and turned the knob.

The heavy steel door emitted a high, thin squeal as she slowly opened it, revealing a dark cavern below. She reached out one hand to search for the light switch, finding it on the wall to the left of the door. She flipped the switch and light flooded the cellar.

"Patrick?" Levi called out, moving directly behind Sarah. "Patrick, are you down there?"

They all waited, but there was no answer. Levi pushed past her and went carefully down the stairs. "Patrick? Please answer me, buddy."

Unlike the messy attic, the contents of the dank cellar were neatly organized. There were cheap plastic shelf units lining the walls; some of the shelves were full of items and others almost empty. She saw canned goods and boxes, along with assorted kitchen appliances, like a toaster oven and a bread machine, in various stages of disrepair.

Sarah watched Levi frantically search for Patrick, ducking down to look under the shelves, his shouts becoming almost theatrical. She felt bad for being so cynical, but she had been sorting through so many lies and deceptions that it was difficult not to be skeptical.

Audrey moved beside Sarah and lightly touched her arm. "How long are we going to stay here?"

She gave Audrey's hand a reassuring pat. "Not too long."

Amy brushed past them and joined Levi on the cellar floor. She began to pull boxes off the shelves and peered inside them.

Sarah found the cellar warmer than she had expected for this time of year. There were two grimy cellar windows on the west wall, but they weren't big enough for a child to climb through, much less an adult.

Levi emerged from a far corner of the cellar. "He's not here."

Sarah's heart sank. If Patrick wasn't here, where was he? She walked down the remaining stairs, determined to see for herself.

"Maybe he really did wander off," Chuck mused as everyone climbed down the stairs. "I don't know what else could have happened to him."

"He'd never do that," Levi reiterated. "Certainly not in February. His car is here and his coat is still in the closet. He has to be here somewhere."

Dorothy rested one hand on a wall. "Maybe he arranged for someone to pick him up. Or he left the inn against his will."

Sarah had imagined those scenarios herself, but they didn't explain why the trail of blood suddenly stopped at the edge of the parlor rug. Could someone really force a bleeding Patrick to his feet, through the house, and out the door without anyone noticing?

There were so many pieces to this mystery, but she was frustrated that she still hadn't figured out the puzzle yet.

"Hey, look what I found," Amy cried, pulling something out of a box.

Sarah walked over, Audrey right behind her. "What is it?"

"I think it's an old picture of Patrick," Amy said.

Sarah took the framed photograph from her and looked down at the young man in a Navy uniform. The man had thick, coal black hair instead of white, but the smile and the green eyes left no doubt as to his identity. "It *is* Patrick."

"Will that help us find him?" Audrey asked.

Amy blushed, looking around her to see if anyone had overheard. "I never said it was a big clue."

Sarah began sorting through the box where Amy had found the picture. It was full of old scrapbooks and other memorabilia. "We'll take this box upstairs with us and see what else we can find."

"I'm freezing," Vonnie said, rubbing her hands up and down her thin arms.

Sarah sorted through the other boxes on the shelves. From the looks of it, Patrick and his predecessors at the inn never threw anything away. Most of the boxes contained junk, like worn kitchen utensils and dishes or assorted tools, but there were a few boxes that held potential clues.

Sarah pulled a box of old newspapers off the shelf. "Can someone carry this box upstairs for me?"

"Sure," Levi said, coming to her aid. He took the box from her and headed up the stairs, setting it near the open cellar door.

After Sarah had searched the last box, she started for the stairs and then noticed something out of the corner of her eye. She bent down to look under one of the shelf units and saw a crumpled yellow and green bag.

"Audrey," she said, pointing to the bag, "can you reach that for me?"

Audrey knelt down on the cellar floor and stretched her arm under the shelf. "Yeah, I got it."

Amy joined them. "Got what?"

"Whatever this is." Audrey handed the bag to Sarah.

Sarah smoothed out the bag and held it up for everyone to see. "This is the potato chip bag that I saw in the pantry yesterday."

Vonnie's eyes widened. "Are you sure?"

"Positive."

As the others gathered around to examine her discovery, Sarah felt a chill of apprehension. One of them had brought it down here. No one said anything, the air around them suddenly growing a lot chillier. The silence continued all the way back to the second floor, where they prepared for Levi to turn off the generator.

Finn whispered to Sarah, "You know what this means, right?"

She nodded. "Someone has had a key to the cellar all along."

"I'll give everyone a few minutes to light candles and stuff," Levi said, pulling on a pair of gloves. "Then I'll shut it off for the night."

The girls stayed with Sarah in her room.

"It's going to happen soon, isn't it," Audrey whispered, looking fretfully up at the ceiling light.

"Yes, but we're ready," Sarah said. "We've got candles lit in both rooms."

Amy shivered, pulling her knees up to her chin. "I'm really cold."

"That's because you're barefoot," Sarah said, reaching out to rub her cold toes. "You'll warm up as soon as you get in bed."

Sarah glanced at the clock, trying to hold back a yawn. It was already past one o'clock in the morning. So much had happened since the chandelier had crashed outside her door. Weariness clouded her mind and she struggled to stay awake long enough to figure out the meaning of the clues she'd found. The antique silver chest. The cellar key. The empty potato chip bag.

But still no Patrick.

Her eyes drooped, but she forced them open again. She needed to stay awake until the girls fell asleep, so she could blow out the candles and go to bed herself.

"Do you think I have time to brush my teeth again?" Amy asked, glancing up at the light.

Audrey frowned at her. "Didn't you already brush them tonight?"

"Yeah, like hours ago." Amy swept her tongue over her front teeth. "I feel like I need to brush them again, but I don't want the lights to go out on me."

"I've lit a candle in your bathroom," Sarah said. "So you won't be in the dark even if the lights do go out."

Amy climbed off the bed and headed for the other room.

After she left, Audrey turned to Sarah. "Can you tell me more about Aunt Jenna?"

"Shouldn't we wait for your sister?"

Audrey shook her head. "She won't care. I started to tell her the story and she told me it was boring."

Sarah tucked one of the pillows under her arm and reclined on the bed. "Where did we leave off?"

Audrey snuggled beside her. "The last thing I remember, Dad and Jenna were going to the river to fish."

"Oh that's right. Well, your dad wanted to have a contest to see who could catch the most fish. The loser would have to clean all the fish for supper. Jenna was pretty good at catching fish and she thought she could win the contest. She didn't know until it was too late that Jason had brought a secret weapon."

"What?"

"Liver."

Audrey scrunched her nose up. "Liver?"

"That's right. A whole carton of chicken livers. It's good bait for catching catfish. Your dad did a lot of research at the library trying to find just the right bait for fishing." Sarah smiled as she remembered how many times Jason had pored over books at the kitchen table. "He didn't tell Jenna or Grandpa Gerry about his plan. He wanted to surprise them."

"Did it work?"

"It sure did," Sarah said. "Those catfish went after that chicken liver almost as soon as he put his line in the water. His bucket was nearly half-full before Jenna even caught her first fish."

Audrey looked thoughtful. "That doesn't seem very fair."

"Your aunt Jenna didn't think so either," Sarah said, "so she came up with a plan—"

The lights suddenly went out, making Audrey gasp.

"It's all right," Sarah assured her. "Levi just shut off the generator."

"I know," Audrey replied, "it just surprised me."

Amy walked back into Sarah's room. "What did I miss?"

"Nothing. Grandma can finish the story tomorrow." Audrey crawled off the bed and headed to the open connecting door. "Can we leave this door open tonight, Grandma?"

"We sure can." Sarah followed the twins to their room and watched Amy set the candle on the nightstand.

"I'll leave the candles lit until you fall asleep," Sarah said, tucking the covers around them, "but remember, if you wake up in the middle of the night, just call out to me and I'll light a candle right away so you can see."

Audrey nodded, turned on her side, and closed her eyes. Sarah looked at Amy, who stared up at her. "Are you okay?"

"Sure," Amy said sharply. "Why wouldn't I be?"

Sarah knew Amy tried to act tough sometimes, but she had such a tender heart. "All right." She leaned down to kiss her forehead. "Good night, girls."

"Good night," Amy said and rolled away from her.

Sarah stood staring at the two girls for a long moment and whispered a prayer into the darkness. "Lord, thank you for all my beautiful grandchildren. Bless Amy and Audrey and Thomas and Jonathan. Guide and protect them as they make their way in this world. Amen."

Amy and Audrey had seen a darker glimpse of the world this weekend. Violence and suspicion and fear. Through it all, they'd made her so proud, acting more mature at twelve than some of the adults at times.

When she was certain both girls were asleep, Sarah blew out the candle in their room and retired to her own. She breathed a sigh of relief when she finally climbed into her bed, pulling the quilt up to her shoulders. Then she leaned over and blew out the candle on her nightstand, hoping that a peaceful night lay ahead of her.

CHAPTER FOURTEEN

T he next morning, the guests gathered in the dining room while Vonnie prepared breakfast. Despite the late night, Sarah had awakened before dawn to review all the documents in the antique chest. And she had found something that changed everything.

A letter from Finn Hawkins to Patrick Maguire.

She dipped her fingertips into the pocket of her cardigan, feeling the edges of the letter.

Her gaze moved over the room, watching everyone. The twins sat at the table with Bella between them. They were each making silly faces, vying for the giggling baby's attention. Finn was at the table too, his face buried in the same newspaper he'd read yesterday. Chuck and Dorothy were helping Vonnie in the kitchen while Levi and Natalie stood talking by the large bay window.

"It looks a lot better out there today," Natalie said as she peered out the window. The light accentuated the dark circles under her eyes. "Maybe they'll be able to clear the roads soon."

Levi turned to her. "The wind and snow have both picked up again. If the county tries to clear the roads now, the blowing snow will just drift over them and shut them down right away again."

Natalie bit her bottom lip, her bloodshot gaze fixed on the snowy landscape. "But what if it never stops blowing? We can't stay stuck here forever."

"Nothing is forever," Levi said.

But Natalie didn't seem to hear him or, if she did, chose not to reply.

Sarah walked into the kitchen. "Can I help you with anything?" she asked Vonnie.

Vonnie stood at the stove stirring a pan of scrambled eggs, her face red from the heat. "Yes, you and Dorothy could set the table."

Sarah walked over to the cupboard and retrieved a stack of plates while Dorothy gathered napkins and silverware. As Sarah walked back into the dining room, she wondered when she should ask Finn about the letter.

"Is breakfast almost ready?" Audrey asked. "I think Bella's getting hungry."

"Almost." Sarah began placing plates on the table. She had to reach around Finn, who didn't move, when she set a plate in front of him.

Dorothy followed her, carefully placing a fork, knife, and spoon at each place. Vonnie and Chuck entered the room carrying bowls of scrambled eggs, a platter of bacon, and a plate stacked with buttered toast.

"Breakfast is ready," Vonnie announced.

Everyone began to gather at the table. When Sarah sat down, the letter slipped out of her pocket and landed on the floor. Before she could grab it, Natalie bent down and picked it up, her gaze landing on the front of the envelope.

"Here, you dropped...wait...this is addressed to Patrick," Natalie said, looking from the envelope to Sarah. "Why do you have it?"

"I found it in the attic," Sarah said. "I thought it might shed some light on Patrick's disappearance."

Before she could stop her, Natalie pulled the letter out of the envelope and began to read it aloud.

"Dear Mr. Maguire," Natalie began, "this is my final offer to purchase the Red Clover Inn, take it or leave it. If you're smart, you'll take it or reap the consequences..." Her voice trailed off as her gaze moved to the bottom of the letter. "It's from Mr. Hawkins."

Finn lowered the newspaper to find everyone staring at him. "Is this a joke?"

"It's no joke." Natalie handed him the letter. "That's your signature, isn't it?"

He quickly scanned the letter, a dark flush creeping up his neck. He remained silent.

"Oh, give it up already." Chuck set the bacon platter on the table with a loud thump. "You're cooked. Just tell us why you didn't mention it before."

"Because it's none of your business," Finn said, reaching for a few strips of bacon before picking up his newspaper once more.

"Are you nuts?" Levi said. "Patrick is missing after you send him a threatening letter and it's none of our business?"

"I made no threat of any kind in that letter," Finn said, his attention fixed on a back page article.

Sarah leaned forward. "Then what did you mean by 'reap the consequences'?"

"It's a common phrase," Finn replied, his fingers tightening on the newspaper and crinkling the edges. "Business decisions have consequences. That's Economics 101. Dorothy was in the banking business; she can tell you the same thing. Just ask her."

"Don't drag me into this," Dorothy told him. "I didn't write that letter."

A slow smile spread across Levi's face. "Looks like you've been caught red-handed, Hawkins. Your trying to weasel out of it only makes you look more guilty."

Finn slammed the newspaper down on the table. "Or someone wants to make me look guilty." He stared at Sarah.

"Why didn't you tell anyone you wanted to buy the inn?" Sarah asked.

"I don't normally share my business with the general public." Finn picked up his fork. "And I don't intend to start now."

Without another word, Finn reached for a bowl of scrambled eggs. For a moment, everyone just watched him fill his plate.

Then Bella held one chubby arm toward Finn's plate and made a loud, gurgling noise.

Finn looked up at Natalie. "Better feed your kid. I'm not sharing."

The food tasted like sawdust in Sarah's mouth, but she ate every bite, knowing she would need her energy for another long day trapped at the inn.

"Scrambled eggs and bacon," Chuck said with an awkward chuckle. "This is like déjà vu all over again."

No one laughed.

Finn's jaw worked those eggs like they were made of granite, his gaze never leaving his newspaper. Dorothy cleared her throat a few times but didn't speak. Natalie stared down at her plate blankly, only looking up when Bella let out an urgent yelp demanding more scrambled eggs to be spooned into her mouth.

Sarah could see the others casting furtive glances at Finn. The night she'd arrived, when he'd insisted on speaking with Patrick in private, he must have been talking about his plans to purchase the inn.

When everyone finally finished breakfast, they made their way into the parlor. Finn cornered Sarah almost immediately.

"I know you think you've solved Patrick's disappearance," Finn said, his voice low and urgent, "but you're wrong. I'm not the only one here with a secret, you know."

"What do you mean?"

"I mean, instead of trying to frame me, why don't you go after the guy Patrick fired the night he disappeared? I heard

Patrick fire Levi Friday night. He stormed out of here but not before telling Patrick he'd be sorry."

Sarah remembered hearing a door slam late Friday night. Had that been Levi leaving in a huff?

Or maybe he hadn't left at all.

There was no way to know if Levi had driven to the inn from Hartford on Saturday morning. His saying so might have been a ruse to give himself an alibi when Patrick turned up missing. Perhaps Patrick was stuffed in Levi's car on some snow-packed country road.

"Why didn't you tell me all this before?" Sarah asked softly.

"Because I thought it might be more interesting to see if Levi came clean himself. The fact that he hasn't speaks volumes, don't you think?"

Sarah didn't say anything as Finn walked away, announcing that he was headed out to the back porch for a smoke. She walked into the library, needing some time to process what Finn had just told her.

From her vantage point, she could easily see the rest of the guests. Vonnie, Chuck, and Levi sat huddled at the game table. Natalie stood alone by the window, staring out at the blizzard. Audrey played with Bella on the floor while Amy sat by the fire with a book.

The light flickered, something Levi had warned them would happen whenever the generator was on. He had fired it up again so Vonnie could cook breakfast, but he must have forgotten to shut it off. They couldn't afford to waste precious gasoline, especially with the storm worsening out-side. The electricity could be out for days.

Sarah walked over to the game table. When Vonnie and Chuck saw her approach, they got up and moved to the fire-place.

"Should I take that personally?" Sarah asked, sitting down at the table with Levi.

"Who knows?" He leaned back in the chair.

"I was just thinking we should turn off the generator as soon as Finn returns from his smoke break," Sarah said. "We don't want to waste any more fuel than necessary."

He snapped his fingers. "Oh yeah. I meant to do that after breakfast." He leaned forward. "So what are we going to do about Finn?"

"What do you mean?" she asked.

"Should we lock him up or something? We could put him in the cellar and, you know, feed him and stuff until the po-lice can get here."

Levi sounded sincere—but the best liars usually did. She didn't know if he was trying to con them, but she suspected he wasn't quite what he seemed.

"So you think that because of the letter…?"

"Of course. Patrick obviously refused to sell the inn and 'reaped' the consequences."

Sarah knew it would be all too easy to blame Finn and declare the mystery solved. The letter did sound threaten-ing, even if Finn hadn't meant it that way. Yet she knew Patrick was having money problems, so it was hard for her to believe that he would turn down a legitimate offer to buy the inn.

And hurting Patrick wasn't a good negotiation tactic— no matter how easy it was to imagine Finn doing just that.

"Well?" Levi prodded. "I think Chuck and I could subdue him. There's some rope in the shed. . . . "

"The letter *is* suspicious," Sarah admitted, "but I think we should wait and see if anything else comes up."

Levi shrugged and rose out of the chair. "I think that's a mistake. If you need more proof, there's always Harvey."

She blinked. "Harvey?"

"Harvey Pittman. Ask Finn. They're what you might call 'business partners.'"

Levi walked away without another word. Sarah went over to the front desk and began quietly opening drawers and digging through them.

Bingo.

In the bottom desk drawer was a letter from Harvey Pittman, dated two weeks ago. She pulled out the letter, noting the return address was from a government agency. She quickly scanned the typewritten letter.

Dear Mr. Maguire,

I want to inform you that the Red Clover Inn once again failed to pass inspection by the Connecticut Department of Public Safety. A formal letter will follow at a later date, but I thought it might be advantageous for you to have this information now so you can begin making the appropriate arrangements to repair the problems. As I told you during my latest tour of your establishment, the Red Clover has numerous fire and safety code violations. Please feel free to contact me if you have any questions.

Sincerely,
Harvey Pittman

She placed the letter back in the envelope just as the computer on the desk blinked and the screen went dark. She looked up, realizing the electricity had gone off. She saw Finn back in the parlor, pacing in front of the fireplace.

"Find anything interesting?"

She jumped and turned around to see Levi standing behind her. He shed his gloves and unzipped his coat. She had been so preoccupied about Finn and Harvey, she hadn't heard him come in from turning off the generator.

"Yes, I did."

"Patrick and Harvey had a long, fruitful relationship." He pulled his hat off, his hair flopping over his face. "Until the last few weeks anyway."

She had gathered that much from the way Mr. Pittman had signed off on the letter. And she had read between the lines. "So Patrick was paying bribes to keep those safety code violations a secret?"

Levi nodded. "That's right. Repairs to an old place like this would have cost Patrick a fortune—much more than those bribes. But Patrick eventually ran out of money and Pittman threatened to close him down."

"And Finn knew about all of this?"

"Yeah, we both did. Pittman was here the other night. Dorothy overheard him demanding money from Patrick on the day she arrived at the inn. It scared her. She didn't know if she should call the police and asked our advice. Guess who convinced her not to do it?"

"Finn?"

"That's right."

Finding that letter had opened an ugly can of worms involving Levi, Patrick, Finn, and now Harvey Pittman and Dorothy. "So that's why Finn was pressuring Patrick to sell the inn," Sarah said slowly. "He knew the state was going to close this place down until it was up to code."

"Patrick told me Finn is in the business of flipping real estate. He thought he could buy the inn cheap, make the repairs, and sell it for a lot more money."

Sarah wondered how Patrick's disappearance played into all of this. It wouldn't help Finn, who needed Patrick to sell the inn to him. The slow grind of the legal system would tie up the inn for years unless Patrick was found. But just because it didn't make sense for Finn to harm Patrick didn't mean he was innocent. Most criminals didn't think before they acted, even if it was against their own best interest.

She met Levi's gaze, trying to read his thoughts. "Anything else you want to share with me?"

"What do you mean?" Levi asked warily.

"Never mind." Sarah walked back into the parlor. She had given him the opportunity. Now it was time to see if he would come clean.

Levi's footsteps sounded behind her. "No, Sarah, tell me." His raised voice made everyone look up at them. "What did you mean by that?"

She turned around to face him. "I mean, we all have secrets, Levi."

Natalie's brow furrowed as she rose slowly from her chair. "What secrets?"

"It's nothing," he said with a dismissive wave. "Nothing important."

"Patrick was assaulted and might be dead now," Sarah said. "Don't you think it's important that we know you spent some time in prison?"

Natalie gasped as all the color drained from Levi's face. "How did you know?" he asked.

"Your tattoo, for one."

His gaze wandered toward his shoulder. "I don't have a tattoo."

"I saw it," she said, walking over to him and tapping the flannel sleeve below his left shoulder. "The other night when the lights went out and you were wearing a T-shirt. It didn't look like a professional tattoo. I've seen something like it before—one of the busboys at my favorite coffee shop in Maple Hill, working there as a condition of his probation."

Dorothy set down her knitting. "Is this true, Levi?"

"Yeah, I have a tattoo," Levi said. "That still doesn't prove anything."

"And I found this." Sarah pulled another piece of paper from her pocket. "It was included with some documents I found in the attic."

He took the paper from her. His jaw tightened as he read the letter. "It's from my probation officer."

Sarah nodded. "It states that you are required to be employed as a condition of your probation. I'm sure it's not easy to find a job when you have a prison record."

Levi handed the letter back but wouldn't meet her gaze. "It's not. I've lost two jobs already. My PO said this one was my last chance or I'd be stuck doing community service."

Levi glanced over at Natalie, who stared at him with her mouth agape. "It was no big deal," he said. "I went joyriding with my neighbor's car on my eighteenth birthday. I was going too fast around a curve and hit another car."

"Joyriding in your neighbor's car?" Finn echoed. "Isn't that what the police call theft?"

Levi scraped a hand across his whiskers. "Yeah, all right. I messed up. And I know what you're all thinking," Levi said, looking around the room, "but you're wrong. I didn't hurt Patrick." His eyes narrowed. "And there's no way anyone here can prove I did."

CHAPTER FIFTEEN

arah sat alone in the library, enjoying the warmth of the noonday sun on her face. The snow had finally let up, at least for now, and the gray clouds had parted. She could hear the scrape of a metal blade against cement and glanced out the window.

Finn, Levi, and Chuck had been taking turns shoveling the sidewalk, each working for a fifteen-minute interval before coming inside to hand off the shovel. Finn was out there now, trying to unearth their buried cars. He'd made quite a lot of progress since the last time she had looked. She could now see most of her silver Grand Prix.

Sarah turned back to the old scrapbook in her lap. She had found four scrapbooks in the cellar, all of them documenting the history of the Red Clover Inn. That history was by no means complete, with several years missing between the founding of the inn in 1890 and the current year.

Still, Sarah found it fascinating.

As far as she could tell, there were no other crimes reported in the history of the inn. One of the scrapbooks did contain a series of articles collected by an apparent crime buff, chronicling the decades-old adventures of a master forger in the Hartford area who had even forged the mayor's signature on several legal documents. Other articles included a British Bonnie and Clyde duo accused of robbing several banks and a jewelry thief who left behind a red rose for each of his victims.

The scrapbooks also contained some national news, such as articles pertaining to World War I and World War II, along with news of local veterans. She looked for a Maguire among the names, wondering if she might find one of Patrick's relatives. But she didn't recognize any names in any of the articles she had read so far.

And she still had two scrapbooks to go.

People were keeping their distance from her, most of them wary of any question she asked, no matter how mundane.

Sarah tried not to let it bother her, aware that she couldn't make friends with people at the same time she was questioning them about a possible crime. At least none of them was outwardly hostile.

She closed the scrapbook on her lap with a sigh of exasperation. She hadn't found anything about Patrick or any of the current guests. As she reached for the next scrapbook, she reminded herself to take time to read every word of the various articles and clippings, hoping to find some nugget that would lead her in the right direction.

The rest of the group sat at the table playing games, except for Levi, who paced back and forth between the parlor and the library. Everyone was keeping some distance from him now, especially Natalie.

Audrey sat in a corner chair near the window, keeping Bella occupied with a small purple teddy bear that Natalie had dug out of her diaper bag. Amy stood over Dorothy's shoulder as the older woman explained the game to her.

Sarah turned her attention back to the scrapbook. It spanned decades and detailed all the local events in Hartford and the surrounding area. There were photographs from an Independence Day parade and a local flower show, as well as results from the county fair and news about various charity events and auctions.

This scrapbook provided a nice slice of regional history as well and had been added to throughout the years. She turned to the end of the book, wondering what Patrick had considered important enough to include, but the last item added to the scrapbook was dated ten years ago. She now realized there were no current articles or photographs in the other scrapbooks either.

According to the deed, Patrick had purchased the inn about ten years ago. Either he didn't know about the scrapbooks or hadn't deemed them important enough to keep up to date. The chance of her finding any clues in them was dwindling and she was starting to run out of time to solve this case.

Finn walked into the parlor, brushing the snow off his hair. "What's for lunch?"

Vonnie glanced at her watch. "Is it that time already?"

"Yep," Finn replied. "There's still a lot of snow left to shovel. It won't do us any good for the county to clear the roads if we can't get out of the driveway."

"You really should let us take turns cooking," Dorothy said to Vonnie. "I'm not the best cook in the world, but I can make a good sandwich."

Vonnie patted the woman's shoulder. "Don't worry about it—I love to cook. Being in the kitchen is one of my favorite things."

"My wife's always been a great cook." Chuck rubbed his stomach. "The only problem for me is that I've always been a great eater!"

The mood had lightened with the weather. And why not? When the roads were cleared, someone was going to get away with a possible murder. A sense of urgency filled Sarah and she realized she needed to start pushing people a bit harder to reveal what they knew about the crime.

Sarah began reading one of the articles in the scrapbook.

It comes as no surprise that Paulette Remmer is this year's winner of the state fair pie contest with her blueberry rhubarb pie. Mrs. Remmer's baking prowess is known far and wide, especially to her guests at the Red Clover Inn near Hartford...

Paulette Remmer. That sounded so familiar. It took her a moment before she remembered. Paulette's peach cobbler. That was Vonnie's mother's recipe. And she had mentioned the Remmer cousins when talking about her mother's hometown in New Jersey.

It had to be the same woman.

Sarah's fingers clutched the edges of the scrapbook. She checked the date of the newspaper article, July 20, 1968, and did a quick mental calculation.

It all fit.

Natalie abandoned the game and walked over to the window. "It looks like the drifts are smaller now, doesn't it? I think the sun is melting them."

"That sun isn't melting anything," Finn said, rubbing his hands together in front of the fireplace.

Natalie kept staring out at the snow. "Maybe we'll even be able to leave this afternoon."

Several of them turned to look out the window.

"Those drifts sure don't look smaller to me," Chuck said. "But at least we've got most of the sidewalks cleared."

"The driveway is next," Finn said. "If we're lucky we might be out of here by tomorrow."

Natalie's shoulders slumped. "Not until tomorrow? Seriously?"

"If we're lucky," Finn said. "Then we'll never have to see each other again."

Sarah closed the scrapbook and stood up. "Until that time comes, we're stuck with each other. So why don't we have lunch?"

Amy looked over at her. "But the game isn't over yet."

"It can wait," Chuck said, pushing back his chair. "My stomach can't."

As they all moved to the dining room, Sarah followed Vonnie into the kitchen. "What can I do to help?"

"With the electricity going on and off, I don't trust what's left in the fridge, so I'm just making peanut butter and jelly sandwiches," Vonnie said. "And I'm going to break open a bag of cookies. I suppose you can help if you want."

Sarah reached for the bread and spread out several slices along the clean countertop. "Tell me more about your mother."

Vonnie stilled. "My mother?"

"Yes. You mentioned she's in New Jersey now. Did she always live there?"

"Uh...yes."

Sarah watched her pull a jar of peanut butter from the cupboard and open it. "Did she have a job there?"

"She was a housewife." Vonnie's brow crinkled as she looked over at Sarah. "Why this sudden interest in my mother?"

"I was just reading an old newspaper article about her."

"Really?"

"She won first place in the pie contest at the state fair. The Connecticut state fair."

The butter knife slipped in Vonnie's hand and clattered onto the counter. She quickly picked it up again. "It must be another Paulette Remmer."

"I don't think so. Especially since a Paulette Remmer once owned the Red Clover Inn. That's just too much of a coincidence."

She watched Vonnie slap peanut butter onto a slice of bread.

"Now I know why you seem so at home in this kitchen," Sarah continued. "You must have been here somewhere in your teens when your mother ran the inn."

Vonnie looked up. "I was fourteen."

Sarah waited, but she didn't say anything else. She opened a jar of grape jelly and began spreading it over the remaining bread slices.

"Why didn't you tell anyone you used to live here?" Sarah asked.

"The past is the past. I like to keep it that way."

"Or maybe you know it gives you a motive to hurt Patrick," Sarah said. "How long have you known him?"

"Ten years." Vonnie made a diagonal slice through each sandwich. "We've missed the place and wanted to see if he'd consider selling it back to us."

Finn spoke from the doorway. "So you were my competition."

Sarah stepped back, wondering how long he had been listening.

Vonnie didn't acknowledge him. She placed the sandwiches on a platter and headed for the dining room. "It's time to eat."

Sarah and Finn paused for a beat, exchanging a glance before they followed her to the dining room, only to find everyone headed back to the parlor.

"Where are we going?" Sarah asked Audrey.

"Vonnie said we're eating in the parlor so they can finish their game."

Something told Sarah that wasn't the only game Vonnie wanted to play. The parlor and library were much larger than the dining room. There were a lot more distractions to hide behind if Sarah kept asking difficult questions.

When they reached the parlor, Natalie walked over to the front window. "I think the snow really is starting to melt." She placed her fingertips against the windowpane. "There's water on the glass."

"It's condensation," Finn said. "A warm room plus a cold window equals condensation. It's basic junior high science."

Bella started to fuss in Audrey's arms. Natalie blinked at the noise and turned away from the window. "Oh sorry." She walked over to Audrey. "What's wrong?"

"I don't know," Audrey replied, bouncing Bella on her knee. "Do you think she might be hungry?"

"I don't think so." Natalie reached out to rub the baby's stomach. "She just had a bottle an hour ago."

Bella's cries grew louder as she stretched her arms toward her mother.

"I think she wants you," Audrey said, starting to hand her over, but Natalie backed away.

"Neither one of us slept much last night, so she's probably just tired." Natalie started walking backward toward the parlor door, her gaze on her daughter. "I'll just go upstairs and get her pacifier and be right back."

As soon as Natalie disappeared from view, Bella began wailing. Audrey looked helplessly at Sarah.

"Will someone shut that kid up already?" Finn shouted over Bella's cries.

Amy hurried over to Audrey, who looked as if she was about ready to start crying herself. "Can I try holding her?"

"Be my guest," Audrey said, handing the baby over.

Amy held the baby awkwardly against her chest as Bella's face turned bright red with her angry sobs. Tears leaked at the corners of Bella's eyes as Amy tried bouncing her up and down.

"You're okay," Amy said, her voice muffled by Bella's wailing. Then she turned to Sarah. "What should I do?"

Sarah moved toward her. "Let me try to settle her down."

Amy let Sarah lift Bella out of her arms and took a step back.

"Hush now," Sarah murmured to the baby, gently rubbing her back. "Your mama will be back soon." Then continued murmuring soft, soothing words to the baby.

Soon Bella's cries settled into subdued sniffling and she allowed Sarah to sit down and rock her.

"How do you do that, Grandma?" Amy asked as she and Audrey stood by the rocking chair.

"I've had lots of practice," Sarah said softly.

"Can I rock her for a little while?" Amy asked.

Although Bella had stopped crying, she squirmed in Sarah's arms and looked like she was on the verge of fussing again. "Soon, Amy. Let's wait until Natalie comes back. Bella gets upset when she doesn't see her mom."

Dorothy walked over to them. "We're about to start a game of Pictionary. Would you two girls like to play?"

"Not me," Audrey said, reaching out to smooth Bella's wispy brown hair.

Amy looked at Bella and back at Dorothy. "I guess I will."

"I'll help you if you need it," Dorothy said, walking with her to the game table.

As the other guests began to play, Audrey pulled a chair closer to Sarah. "I think Bella's finally starting to fall asleep," she whispered.

Sarah lightly rubbed the baby's back and felt her small body relax more deeply against her. She kept rocking back and forth, almost certain Bella would be fast asleep by the time Natalie returned with the pacifier.

Audrey leaned forward. "So, Aunt Jenna found out my dad brought the secret chicken liver bait. Then what?"

Sarah smiled, somewhat surprised that Audrey was so intrigued by the story. Then again, Sarah had always loved hearing stories about her father and mother when she was a youngster. It was hard to imagine your parents as children, which made stories from their childhood all the more fascinating.

"Well, Jenna knew she was going to lose the contest, especially when Jason refused to share his chicken liver bait with her. The worst part was that he was catching so many catfish that she was afraid she'd be cleaning fish all night long." The baby's soft breathing told Sarah that Bella was finally asleep. She kept her voice low, not wanting to wake her. "So she came up with a plan. Jenna figured that if Jason couldn't find her, then he couldn't make her clean all his fish. But she needed to find a good hiding place."

Audrey smiled. "I bet there are lots of good hiding places on the mountains."

"Oh, there are. Caves and hollow logs. But Gerry had made a rule that the kids were always to stay together when they went fishing and not wander away from the river. Jenna knew if she broke that rule, she'd be in big trouble."

"Did Aunt Jenna hide in the river?"

"No," Sarah chuckled softly. "The water was crystal clear, so Jason would have seen her there if she'd tried. It was only a few feet deep and barely reached her waist."

Audrey shook her head. "It doesn't sound like there was any good place to hide by the river."

"Oh, but there was," Sarah told her. "A wonderful place under a giant fir tree. The branches hung so low to the ground that she was sure Jason would never find her."

Audrey's eyes widened with surprise and admiration. "That does sound like a great hiding place."

"While Jason was busy catching another fish," Sarah continued, "Jenna snuck behind him and hid under the tree.

Her plan was to stay there just long enough for Jason to go looking for her, then she was going to pour his big bucket of catfish back into the river and head back to the campsite with the fish she'd caught."

"I bet my dad was really mad when he saw his empty bucket."

Bella stirred slightly, rubbing her face against Sarah's sweater before settling down once more.

"She never got to empty his bucket because something happened that wasn't part of her plan. Jenna settled down on the soft pine needles to wait but was so tired that she fell asleep."

Before Sarah could continue, Natalie walked back into the parlor carrying an empty plastic baby bottle. "I can take her now."

"Are you sure?" Sarah asked. "I don't mind holding her."

"I'm sure." Natalie gently took the sleeping baby from Sarah. "I just realized why she was fussing before. I forgot to give her the special drops for her colic. I put some in her bottle, so now I just need to add a little warm milk to it." She carried Bella out of the parlor. "I'll be right back."

Sarah watched them go and glanced over at Levi and saw him watching Natalie too. She turned back to Audrey. "Now, where were we?"

"Aunt Jenna had just fallen asleep under the tree."

"Oh that's right. Well, when she finally woke up—"

Finn rapped his knuckles on the game table. "Hey, kid, are you trying to lose this game for us? You didn't draw anything."

Sarah looked toward the game table to see them all looking at Amy.

"Sorry," Amy said and pushed the drawing pad away from her. "I didn't realize time was running out."

"Let's call that a practice round," Dorothy said. "Hey," Chuck protested as Dorothy erased his team's points from the score pad. "That's not fair."

Vonnie patted his arm. "Oh, Chuck, it's just a game." Then she froze. "Do you hear that?"

Everyone fell silent until the only sounds in the room were the ticking of the mantle clock and the crackling of the fire.

"Hear what?" Dorothy asked at last.

Levi stood up. "It sounds like a car."

Sarah strained her ears and heard the muffled roar of an engine. She slowly rose to her feet.

Hope lit Vonnie's face. "Is it the snowplow? Are they clearing the roads?"

Finn rushed over to the window, pulling the drapes far apart. "I don't believe it." Then he turned around. "It's Natalie. She's making a run for it!"

CHAPTER SIXTEEN

Sarah hurried to the window. "That can't be Natalie!"

"It is," Finn replied as everyone gathered around the window. "That's her car and that's her behind the wheel. Man, she looks intense."

"Where's Bella?" Sarah watched the green Ford Focus battle the snow drifts as it slowly inched its way down the long driveway. The roar of the car's engine grew louder every time the wheels started to spin.

"She's got to be in the car with her," Vonnie said.

"What does she think she's doing?" Chuck exclaimed. "She'll never make it out of here in that car."

Levi moved closer to the window, resting his palm on the cold glass. "Even if she makes it out of the driveway, the roads will be impassable. She'll freeze to death out there if we don't stop her."

"Then let's go," Chuck said, leading the way out of the parlor.

They all hurried to the kitchen where Finn, Levi, and Chuck had left their coats after shoveling snow.

The men donned their coats and gloves, and Finn and Chuck followed Levi outside while Sarah and the others watched them from the kitchen window. Sarah didn't understand what would make Natalie do something like this.

"Is she even wearing a coat?" Dorothy asked, squinting at the car. "I can't tell."

Neither could Sarah. Natalie was gunning for the road, her bare hands curled around the steering wheel as the rear end of the small car shimmied its way forward through the snow.

The men hurried over the shoveled walkway, but their progress slowed considerably when they reached the drifts in the driveway.

They trudged through the snow, Levi leading the way and cutting a narrow trail through the waist-high drifts, following the thin tracks the car's tires had left. Fortunately, Natalie's car wasn't moving anymore, now high-centered on a large drift. But she kept gunning the engine, the tires spitting snow into the air.

"Where's she going, Grandma?" Audrey asked, her eyes wide with confusion as she looked out the window. "Why is Natalie trying to leave?"

"I don't know."

Now that Sarah thought about it, Natalie had been acting a little strange ever since breakfast. She had kept commenting that the snow was melting and the roads would be clear soon. Sarah had assumed it was simply wishful thinking, but now she wondered if the girl was becoming delusional. No one in his right mind could believe a compact car would make it through such large drifts.

After several minutes, Levi finally reached the car with Chuck and Finn close behind him. Levi pounded on the driver's side window, but Natalie ignored him, the tires still spinning as she gunned the engine some more. Sarah could see Finn and Chuck try to move out of the way as the spinning tires sprayed them with snow.

Sarah watched the men talking to Natalie through the closed window. After what seemed an eternity, Chuck and Finn returned to the inn, both of them covered in snow. Vonnie poured a soda for each of them. Sarah was about to suggest coffee instead but then remembered the generator was off.

"What did she say?" Dorothy asked the men.

"She won't come in," Chuck said, brushing snow out of his hair. "She wouldn't even look at us. It was like we weren't even there."

"Then why is Levi still out there?" Vonnie asked as she set the two soda glasses in front of the men.

Finn curled his red, stiff fingers around his glass. "Because he's determined to play Sir Galahad or die trying— which might not take too long in this weather."

Dorothy's worried gaze moved back to the window. "He'll have frostbite for sure if he stays out there too much longer. At least Natalie can run the heat in her car. She and the baby will be toasty warm—until she runs out of gas."

Sarah knew Levi was young enough to let his heart rule over his head. She watched as Natalie's car suddenly shot ahead a few feet and got stuck in another large drift. Levi waded through the snow to catch up with it again.

Sarah moved toward the door. "I'm going out there."

"But, Grandma," Amy protested, following her. "It's too cold."

Sarah patted her thin shoulder. "I'll be fine. Someone has to talk sense into that girl."

"Here." Finn shrugged out of his heavy winter coat and handed it to her, along with his leather gloves. "Take these. You're going to need them."

Sarah didn't know what to say, surprised by such a kind gesture coming from Finn. "Thank you."

She pulled on the coat and gloves, knowing they didn't have a moment to lose. If Natalie managed to make it out of the driveway, she and her car could end up buried in a deep ditch beyond where they could help her.

Frosty air greeted her as she walked through the screened porch and her lungs ached at the stark contrast to the warm kitchen air. Snow lay like sifted flour along the edges of the green all-weather carpet and a rusty coffee can full of sand and cigarette butts sat next to the screen door. She waited a moment to adjust to the sudden change in temperature and walked outside.

The full force of the frigid wind hit her and almost bowled her off her feet. She steadied herself before starting to follow the snowy path forged by the men. The frosty air nipped at her nose and throat as she worked her way forward. Natalie's car had seemed a lot closer from the window.

Sarah glanced over her shoulder to see the others watching her from the house. Amy had her face pressed against the glass and waved when she saw Sarah looking at them. Sarah waved back, her hand encased in one of Finn's big brown gloves. It might look ridiculous, but the thick padding was keeping her hands warm—for now.

Even if she hadn't been able to see Natalie's car, she could simply follow the loud roar of the engine. Natalie continued to hit the gas pedal, as chunks of snow and ice flew from the rear tires. As Sarah got closer to the car, she edged toward one side to avoid the flying snow.

Levi still stood by the driver's window, bending just low enough to peer inside. She could see his mouth moving, but Natalie had kept the window up, so she wasn't sure if the girl could even hear him.

To Sarah's surprise, the cold air was already starting to slow her down, her legs growing stiff as she pushed through the snow. She held a glove over her nose and mouth to warm the cold air she breathed in.

One thing was clear to her from this short trek to Natalie's car: if Patrick had left the inn on foot Friday night, there was no way he could have survived the walk to the nearest farm a mile away, especially if he was injured.

Relief showed on Levi's windburned face when Sarah finally reached the car. "Maybe you can talk some sense into her. She won't listen to me."

"You should go back inside now," Sarah told him.

Sarah glanced at Natalie in the driver's seat, seeing the tear streaks on the girl's pale cheeks. Her hands gripped the steering wheel, her knuckles as white as snow as she steered her way to nowhere.

Whatever the reason for her escape attempt, Sarah knew they were wasting time out here. She needed to convince Natalie to get out of the car and come inside.

Sarah tapped on the window. "Natalie? It's Sarah. Let me in."

The girl shook her head, still revving the engine. Sarah waited for the noise to die down and shouted. "Bella is scared."

Natalie turned to her and mouthed something Sarah couldn't understand.

"I can't hear you. Please let me in the car so we can talk."

Natalie unlocked the doors, and Sarah opened the car door behind Natalie and slipped into the backseat, welcoming the warmth that enveloped her. "Thank you, Natalie."

"Take Bella with you," Natalie said through her sobs. "I don't deserve to have her."

"Yes, you do," Sarah said bluntly. "But Bella needs you to take her back to the inn. It's not safe for either one of you out here."

"You don't understand. I can't face another night in the dark. I keep hearing noises and footsteps. ..."

"We have candles and flashlights," Sarah reminded her.

"It doesn't matter," Natalie cried. "I don't know who to trust anymore. Maybe Levi's the one who hurt Patrick. Or Finn did. Or Dorothy. Or Chuck. Or Vonnie. Or even you. I just can't take this anymore."

Natalie crumpled against the steering wheel, her sobs shaking her body. Sarah got out of the backseat and opened the driver's door, putting her arms around the girl. "Let's go inside."

"No," she cried.

"Running away won't solve anything, Natalie. You'll never forgive yourself if something happens to Bella, especially when she needs you the most."

"I'm not a good mom," she sobbed, finally letting Sarah pull her from the car without resistance. Then Sarah unbuckled Bella from her car seat and lightly draped her blanket around her face to shield it from the wind.

"I never should have brought Bella out here," Natalie sobbed. "She'd be better off without me."

"Nonsense," Sarah told her as they turned toward the inn. She circled one arm around Natalie's waist, keeping a firm hold on the girl in case she tried to bolt for the car. "You're tired, that's all."

Natalie shook her head. "You don't understand."

Sarah didn't ask her to explain. Natalie wasn't rational at the moment and Sarah didn't want to unwittingly push the wrong buttons. The most important thing now was getting Natalie into the house.

When she was almost there, Finn and Chuck emerged from the screened porch to help her escort Natalie the rest of the way. The men practically carried the girl into the house while Sarah followed, her chest heaving from the exertion of fighting all that snow and carrying Bella.

"Are you all right?" Audrey asked, her face drawn with concern when Sarah finally entered the kitchen.

"I'm fine," Sarah replied, allowing Vonnie to take Bella out of her arms. The baby didn't seem harmed by the experience, all warm and cozy in her pink snowsuit.

Sarah's muscles had turned to rubber and she gratefully slid into the chair that Chuck had placed near the kitchen stove.

"Drink this," Dorothy said, handing her a cup of soda. "The sugar will give you a boost of energy."

Sarah took a sip of the soda. "Thank you."

Natalie sat in a chair beside her, dabbing at her eyes with a tissue. "I'm so sorry. I don't know what came over me."

"Where did you think you were going?" Finn asked.

Natalie looked up at him. "To get help."

Finn shook his head. "Of all the crazy stunts—"

"Not now," Dorothy admonished, brushing a strand of Natalie's hair off her face. "Can't you see the girl's exhausted? She's been caring for a baby this whole time while we've only had to worry about ourselves."

"Bella," Natalie breathed, turning to Vonnie. "Can I hold her?"

"Of course." Vonnie handed her over and Bella smiled when she saw her mother.

Fresh tears flowed from Natalie's eyes. "Oh, my sweet little Bella, I'm so sorry. I didn't mean to hurt…If only he…I never thought.…"

Sarah listened to the broken apology, sensing an undercurrent in Natalie's words.

"You deserve better," Natalie said at last, speaking directly to her daughter. "I'm so sorry for…everything."

"I think you need to rest," Sarah told Natalie, setting her soda aside before helping the girl to her feet. Sarah exchanged glances with Audrey and her granddaughter gently took the baby from Natalie.

"I feel too wired to sleep," Natalie said, her voice breaking on a sob. "Like there's something wrong with me."

"You're exhausted," Vonnie told her. "I used to get that way sometimes when I worked a double shift. It feels like you have electric currents shooting through your body."

Natalie nodded. "That's exactly how it feels."

"Here." Dorothy dug into her pocket and produced an enamel pill case. "The doctor gave me these after Leo died. They're not very strong, but they do help you relax so you can fall asleep."

Natalie hesitated. "But what if Bella starts crying and I don't wake up?"

"We'll bring Bella's crib into our room," Sarah told her, "just for this afternoon. I'm sure the girls will enjoy entertaining her and that way you can have a nice, long nap."

"Yes, please let us take care of her," Audrey begged. "It will be so much fun."

"I guess if you really don't mind." Natalie took the pill from Dorothy and chased it down with a glass of water.

A short while later, they got Natalie settled in her bed and moved the crib to the twins' room. Sarah prepared a bottle for the baby before returning to her room, leaving the connecting door open so she could hear the girls in case they needed help.

Alone at last, she sat down on her bed and breathed a sigh of relief. *Thank you, Lord, for giving me the strength I needed to help Natalie. Please be with her and give her the strength and faith she needs to be a good mother to Bella. Amen.*

The other guests had retired to their rooms for the afternoon too. Sarah knew she should add the latest updates to her notebook, but she was still worn out from venturing outside. She lay back on the bed, her head sinking into the feather pillow.

A few minutes later, Sarah awoke to a light tapping on her shoulder.

"Grandma, are you asleep?"

Sarah opened her eyes and saw Audrey standing beside the bed. "Not yet. Is Bella all right?"

Audrey sat on the bed. "She's fine. Amy's feeding her now."

Sarah sat up in bed, propping the pillows behind her. She relished the warmth of the heavy Grandmother's Puzzle quilt after her foray outside. "So what are you doing?"

"I just can't wait any longer," Audrey said. "You have to tell me what happened to Aunt Jenna."

Sarah smiled as she scooted over to make room on the bed. Audrey climbed under the covers and plumped a pillow under her head. When she was all settled in, Sarah continued the story.

"So Jenna fell asleep under the tree. When she woke up, she went to find your dad. Only he wasn't at the river. And neither was his bucket of catfish."

"Oh no. He must have figured out her plan."

"Even worse. Someone had moved the flags Grandpa Gerry had set out so they could find their way back to the campsite."

"So she was lost there?"

"Well, Jenna didn't think so. First, she headed one way and then another, always finding her way back to their fishing spot when she didn't find the tent."

"Why didn't she call for help?"

"She did, but nobody ever answered her. And then something even worse happened." Sarah leaned over to kiss her forehead. "And I'll have to tell you after our nap."

"Grandma!"

"I'm sorry, dear, but I'm so tired I can't even keep my eyes open. Why don't you try to think of all the things that might have happened while I sleep. Then you can see if you guessed the right one."

"Okay," Audrey said reluctantly, rising off the bed. "It's my turn to feed Bella now anyway. But you have to tell me as soon as you wake up."

"I promise," Sarah said, drifting off as Audrey walked into the other room.

She dreamed of Greylock Mountain and a girl hidden beneath a huge fir tree, calling for help. Only it wasn't Jenna in her dream, it was Amy. She was calling out for help too, but Sarah couldn't find her.

"Grandma!"

Sarah woke up with a start, the clock on the nightstand telling her she'd been asleep for almost two hours. Audrey was standing beside the bed, her freckled face pale.

"What is it?" Sarah sat up in bed. "What's wrong?"

"It's Amy. She's gone."

CHAPTER SEVENTEEN

S arah scrambled out of bed. "What do you mean?"

"I fell asleep after I put Bella down in her crib. When I woke up, Amy wasn't there."

Sarah hurried into the girls' room. Bella slept peacefully in her crib, but Amy wasn't in the bed or anywhere else in the room. Sarah ducked down to look under the bed and pulled open the closet door.

"I've looked everywhere," Audrey cried as she followed Sarah into the bathroom. It was empty too.

Sarah's heart began to pound as she checked the door that led to the hallway. It was still locked, but she noticed something on the floor beside Amy's open backpack.

A cigarette butt.

She bent down to pick it up, recognizing the brand of cigarettes that Finn smoked. Fear tightened in her throat as she bolted out the door.

"Finn Hawkins!" Sarah shouted, half running down the hallway to his room. When she reached it, she pounded her fist against the solid oak door, ignoring the pain it caused her hand.

A moment later, Finn opened the door. "What's going on out here?"

"My granddaughter is gone."

He stepped out into the hallway and closed the door behind him, a move that made Sarah's stomach drop. He couldn't have hurt Amy, she thought to herself. She'd admired his quick wit. Laughed at some of his jokes.

Audrey stood behind her, gripping her arm. Sarah forced herself to take a deep, calming breath.

Finn's sleepy eyes widened. "What are you talking about?"

She held up the crushed cigarette butt with trembling fingers. "I found this in the girls' room. What have you done with her?"

Her shouts and door pounding had drawn the other guests from their rooms. Even Natalie appeared, her eyes heavy with sleep.

"Where is Amy?" Sarah cried, her voice wobbling with anger. She felt like a mama bear protecting her cub, ready to break down that door and search for her granddaughter.

"What's going on out here?" Dorothy asked, looking between Sarah and Finn.

"I can't find Amy," Sarah's voice broke and she sucked in another deep breath to steady herself.

Finn backed away from her. "I didn't take your granddaughter anywhere, Sarah. I've been in my room the whole time."

Levi stepped forward. "I told you we should have locked him in the cellar."

Sarah could sense the group gathering around her and lending their support. She brushed past Finn, throwing his door wide open as she walked into his room. It was as messy as before, but she didn't care, stepping on his papers and books as she searched for her granddaughter.

Finn called after her. "You can't just waltz in here and—"

Sarah ignored him, shoving an empty suitcase out of the way and digging through a pile of blankets in the corner. "Amy? Amy, where are you?"

There was no answer.

She looked everywhere a twelve-year-old girl could possibly be concealed. In the bathroom, the closet, and under the bed. She simply couldn't understand why Finn would do something like this. Had he wanted to scare Sarah off her investigation? If so, it was working. She had rarely been so frightened in her life, to the point where the fear was starting to affect her physically. Her heart pounded out an erratic drumbeat of distress and she had trouble catching her breath.

"Amy, please come out," Sarah cried as she looked frantically around the room.

The image of telling Jason and Maggie that she had lost their daughter flashed through her mind and a sob tore at the back of her throat. She swallowed it back, knowing she couldn't give in to her fears now. Not when Audrey needed her to stay strong.

"She's not here, Sarah," Dorothy said, gently leading her out of the room. "Amy's not here."

"That's what I've been trying to tell you." Finn looked Sarah directly in the eyes. "I didn't take your granddaughter. I didn't hurt her." He stepped closer, his face almost touching hers as he slowly enunciated each word. "I. Don't. Know. Where. She. Is."

She wanted to shake the truth out of him. "Then explain why one of your cigarette butts was in her room!"

"I can't." He raked a hand through his hair. "Someone must have planted it there. Someone like him." He pointed at Levi. "You'd do just about anything to take the heat off yourself, wouldn't you, kid?"

Levi stared him down. "That's crazy."

"Just step onto the screened porch and grab one out of that old coffee can, plant it in Sarah's room." Finn said. "You probably pocketed one this morning when you started the generator back up."

A muscle twitched in Levi's jaw as he took a step toward Finn. "You can't prove that."

Sarah had heard enough. "Just stop! We need to find my granddaughter!"

Natalie reappeared with Bella in her arms.

Dorothy moved toward Sarah, giving her a reassuring hug. "We'll find her. We'll search every room in this inn—starting with mine if we have to—until we find her."

Sarah nodded, reaching for Audrey's hand. There were tears running down Audrey's cheeks as she looked beseechingly at Sarah.

She gave her granddaughter's hand a reassuring squeeze and leaned down to whisper. "Don't worry. We'll find her. God's watching over all of us."

Sarah realized she needed to remember that too and not give in to her fear and panic. Amy had to be somewhere close by. There was nowhere else for her to go. Sarah was determined to find her and, with God's help, she'd do just that.

Chuck led the way down the hallway to Dorothy's room, but there was no sign of Amy there, either. Sarah walked over to Dorothy's bedroom window to look out over the front entrance. There were no small footprints in the snow, just the narrow path they'd forged from the screened porch to Natalie's stranded car. From her high vantage point, she couldn't see Amy inside the Ford Focus. That meant she had to be somewhere in the inn.

What troubled Sarah the most was that Amy wasn't calling out for her. Was she gagged? Or unconscious? *Please, Lord, let Amy be all right. Please protect her and watch over her. I love her so much.*

Sarah didn't stop praying as they searched all the other guests' rooms and the main floor, as well as the cellar and the attic and the shed. Each time they opened a door, Sarah hoped to see Amy standing behind it. Each time, she was disappointed.

"I don't understand," Natalie said after they returned from the shed. "Amy has to be here somewhere. She couldn't just disappear."

Finn, Chuck, and Levi even made another trek out to Natalie's Ford Focus, just to be certain she wasn't inside. They came back empty-handed.

Audrey laid her head on Sarah's shoulder and started sobbing. "Oh Grandma. I'm so scared."

"Hush now," Sarah said softly, rubbing her back. "We'll find her. I promise you we'll find her."

The others stood helplessly by as Audrey cried in Sarah's arms. She didn't know where to look next. It was as if Amy had disappeared into thin air.

Finn cleared his throat. "There is one place we haven't looked yet."

They all turned to stare at him and Sarah found herself hoping he was finally ready to reveal where he had taken Amy. Perhaps he did have a heart after all.

"Where?" Vonnie asked him.

Finn looked at Sarah. "Your room."

Sarah sighed, disappointment sinking its fangs into her. "That was the first place I looked. Why would you think I'd hide my own granddaughter?"

"I didn't say you hid her there," Finn replied, his voice kinder than usual. "But you were pretty frantic when you showed up at my door. Maybe you didn't conduct a thorough search of your own room before you went off gunning for me."

Sarah spun on her heel and headed for her room, determined to show Finn that he was wrong. Then she was going to take Levi up on his offer of locking Finn in the cellar. Maybe if the man spent some time alone in the dank recesses of the inn, he would be ready to reveal what he had done with Amy.

Sarah threw open the door to her room. "See for yourself. Amy's not here."

She couldn't believe they were wasting time like this. Amy was lost and Sarah didn't know where to look next. Maybe they should search the attic and cellar again.

Finn opened the door to the closet and peeked in the bathroom and shrugged his shoulders. "I guess she's not here."

Sarah buried her face in her hands, despair filling her.

Then someone sneezed.

She looked up. The sneeze hadn't come from the people gathered in the hallway. It had come from the bed. Only the bed was empty.

Finn arched a brow in her direction. "I think someone owes me an apology." Then he walked over to the bed and bent down on one knee, lifting the white lace bed skirt. "Olly olly oxen free."

To Sarah's amazement and great relief, Amy slid out from beneath the bed. She rushed over to her granddaughter, pulling the girl into her arms. "Oh Amy! You scared me to death."

"I'm sorry, Grandma," Amy whispered, sounding as if she couldn't breathe.

Sarah loosened her grip, but she continued to hug Amy until it finally sunk in that she had been found safe and sound. Then Sarah held her granddaughter at arm's length, looking her up and down just to make certain she wasn't hurt. She didn't see any scratches or bruises.

"Are you all right?" Sarah asked her. "What happened?"

Amy's gaze fell to the floor. "Do I have to tell you in front of everyone?"

Something in Amy's tone made Sarah's heart sink. "Yes, you do. You gave us all quite a scare."

Amy slowly lifted her gaze until she met Sarah's eyes. "I wanted to hear the story."

"What story?" Sarah asked, the words not quite making sense. She was still caught up in the adrenaline of losing Amy and finding her again.

"The story you were telling Audrey about Dad and Aunt Jenna when they were young. Audrey told me it was a secret story just for her."

It took her a moment to comprehend what Amy was saying. She had assumed Finn or someone else had gone after the girl and Amy had sought refuge in Sarah's room. Now it seemed another picture was emerging, one that had Sarah flummoxed. "You mean you hid under my bed...on purpose?"

Amy nodded.

Sarah closed her eyes, remembering how she had almost attacked Finn when she'd found that cigarette butt in the girls' room. She pulled it from her pocket and held it in front of Amy. "And where did this come from?"

Amy blushed. "I...found it."

"Where?"

"On the screened porch while you were outside trying to get Natalie to come back to the inn. I didn't want to smoke it," Amy said. "I thought the police could use it to get Mr. Hawkins's DNA in case he was able to escape before they could get here."

Finn crossed his arms over his chest. "Great. The whole family's trying to frame me."

Sarah stepped in front of Amy. "I'm not trying to frame anyone," she said softly. "And I do owe you an apology, Mr. Hawkins. I'm very sorry." She turned to the rest of the guests. "Thank you so much for helping me look for Amy. I'm sorry we caused all of this trouble."

"No trouble at all," Dorothy assured her, reaching out to pat her arm. "I'm just glad it all turned out okay."

"So am I," Natalie chimed in, nuzzling the top of Bella's head. "And I owe everyone an apology too. Sorry I flipped out earlier. I haven't been sleeping well since Patrick disappeared and I guess it finally caught up with me."

Vonnie twisted her hands together, a frown tugging at the corners of her mouth. "So you're all just taking this at face value?"

Levi looked at her. "What do you mean?"

"I mean, Sarah was ready to convict Finn of abducting her granddaughter and was even carrying proof around in her pocket." Vonnie jabbed a finger in Sarah's direction. "That cigarette butt almost convinced me he was guilty until Finn called her bluff and searched her room. If Amy here hadn't sneezed, we might be locking Finn in the cellar right now."

Sarah stared at her, amazed that Vonnie could consider her so diabolical. "You think I'd recruit my own granddaughters in some scheme just to accuse one of you?"

Vonnie's gaze narrowed on her. "I think you're as much of a suspect as everybody else in this place, Sarah Hart. Which means you might do almost anything to try and play the innocent."

"Now, Vonnie," Chuck chided, but one glance from his wife made him stop talking.

"I've said my piece," Vonnie moved toward the door. "I just thought we should lay it all out there so Sarah didn't think she could pull one over on us."

Sarah didn't even know how to reply to such a charge. She had been so busy looking for evidence against the rest of them she had never even considered that one of them might suspect her.

"I'd like to finish my nap," Dorothy said, breaking the tension. "Why don't we return to our rooms for a while. I think we could all use a bit of a rest from each other."

Sarah wanted to resolve this conflict with Vonnie, but one look at her granddaughters told her this wasn't the time to do it. Amy's pale face and Audrey's tear-streaked cheeks told her it was time to put her role as a grandmother ahead of her tasks as an amateur sleuth.

"I think that's a good idea," Sarah said softly.

CHAPTER EIGHTEEN

arah sat down on her bed, one granddaughter on either side of her. Now that she had recovered from the shock of losing Amy and finding her again, she wanted to discover what was behind her granddaughter's disappearing act.

"Now, Amy, I want to know why you were hiding under my bed."

Amy slowly looked away. "I already told you, Grandma."

"You told me you wanted to hear the story about Aunt Jenna. But you must have heard me calling for you right away. Why didn't you answer me?"

Amy's eyes fixed on the floor and tears pooled in her blue eyes. "If you want to know the truth, I didn't think you'd really care if I was missing."

The words shocked her. Sarah placed her hand on Amy's shoulder. "Not care? How can you say that?"

Her tone came out sharper than she intended, causing Amy's tears to spill over onto her cheeks. "Please don't be mad at me, Grandma."

Sarah softened her voice. "I'm not mad at you, Amy. I just truly want to understand. When I thought you were missing I was more scared than I've ever been in my life. How can you possibly believe that I don't care about you?"

Amy gulped back a sob. "Because you always let Audrey *do* everything. She gets to hold Bella all the time and hear your stories about Dad and Aunt Jenna. She's your favorite."

Sarah circled her arm around Amy's waist, pulling her in for a hug. Despite the girl's misconception, she was truly distraught. "I don't have favorites," Sarah said gently. "I love all my grandchildren equally."

Amy shook her head in disbelief. "Then why do you always let Audrey stay in your room? Why do you always tell Natalie that Audrey can help with the baby but not me? Why do you always make me apologize to her?"

"Apologize to her?" Sarah echoed. "When did I do that?"

"When I accidentally hit her with that shoe. You didn't make her apologize for sticking her tongue out at me."

The words tumbled out of Amy's mouth so fast Sarah could barely understand her. But one thing was clear—Amy had been feeling left out. When Sarah saw her own behavior through Amy's eyes, she could understand why the girl might feel that way. Perhaps she *had* played favorites. Audrey was always so open and easy to talk to while Amy was so much quieter and reserved. Sarah knew still waters often ran deep and Amy's heartfelt pain was now apparent on her tear-stained face.

Sarah gave her a warm squeeze. "Oh Amy. I'm so sorry. I never meant to exclude you or make you feel bad. If I ever do anything to make you think I'm playing favorites, I want you to tell me right away, okay?"

Amy nodded. "I'm sorry I hid from you, Grandma. I thought I'd get in trouble for hiding under your bed so I didn't say anything when you first started looking for me."

Sarah sat back far enough to see her face. "Why would you think you'd be in trouble?"

"Because I was listening to the secret story."

Sarah shook her head. "It wasn't a secret."

Amy looked over at her sister, who had been unusually quiet during their entire conversation. "Audrey told me it was. She said the story was only for her."

Sarah turned to look at Audrey. "Why would you say such a thing?"

Now it was Audrey's turn to stare down at the floor, her lower lip jutting out. "I don't know."

Sarah sighed, realizing neither of her granddaughters was a perfect angel. Audrey had been tormenting her sister by implying that Sarah had been sharing secrets exclusively with her, all the while telling Sarah that Amy didn't care about hearing the story.

And she'd believed her.

Obviously, Sarah hadn't been a perfect grandmother either, if such a person existed.

"I think we all need a fresh start," Sarah declared. "No more secrets, no more hiding, and no more playing favorites, even if it was unintentional. Deal?"

Amy's face relaxed into a smile. "Deal."

"Deal," Audrey echoed.

Sarah moved back to her chair. "Now, who would like to hear the rest of Aunt Jenna and Jason's story?"

"Me!" Audrey replied, taking a seat on the floor in front of her.

"Me too," Amy said, joining her sister. "But I've only heard bits and pieces of the story so far."

Sarah filled her in from the beginning, taking care to include every detail she'd told Audrey.

"So your aunt Jenna was lost," Sarah said when she'd finally caught Amy up on the story. "Then it started to rain. There's one thing you probably don't know about Aunt Jenna. When she was a little girl, she was terrified of thunder and lightning. Whenever there was a storm, she'd hide under the covers of her bed until it was over. Only there weren't any beds on the mountain and she couldn't find her tent so she did the next best thing."

Sarah paused a moment for dramatic effect. "She hid right back under that big tree. The storm lasted for three hours. When it finally stopped, she came out from under the tree and started searching for the campsite again. This time, she found it, only Jason and Grandpa Gerry weren't there."

"When Jason couldn't find Jenna, he went back to the campsite and told Grandpa Gerry that he'd lost her. They looked all around the river and campsite, calling her name wherever they went."

"Only she couldn't hear them because she was asleep," Audrey said.

Sarah nodded. "That's right. And they couldn't find her anywhere. It was like she had disappeared. What Jenna didn't know was that Grandpa Gerry and Jason decided to drive down the mountain so they could get other people to help with the search. But Grandpa Gerry's truck wouldn't start, so they had to walk down the mountain in the rain."

"How long did that take?" Amy asked.

"About three hours, the same amount of time that Jenna was stuck under that tree. When she finally found her way back to the campsite, nobody was there. But she knew she was going to be in big trouble as soon as they came back. So while Jenna was waiting for them at the camp," Sarah continued, "Grandpa Gerry and Jason finally reached the bottom of the mountain and hitched a ride with someone into Maple Hill. They went to the police station first to arrange a search party and came home to tell me that Jenna was missing."

"That must have been awful," Audrey breathed.

"It was." She bent down and kissed Amy's forehead. "Almost as awful as when I thought Amy was missing. I went to the mountain with Grandpa Gerry and Jason and the search party. The police had even arranged to have a search and rescue dog along to help find her."

"Oh no," Audrey said. "I bet she was in really big trouble if they all went there for nothing."

"Well, not quite nothing," Sarah replied. "We went to the camp first and there was Jenna, cleaning all those catfish that Jason had caught at the river. When she saw us, she said, 'It's about time you all got here. We've got enough fish to feed an army.'"

Amy laughed. "So what happened?"

"We had a fish fry," Sarah replied, laughing along with her. "We couldn't let all those people leave on an empty stomach. Even the dog got some fish."

Amy looked down at the bed. "Did Aunt Jenna get in trouble for hiding?"

"Grandpa Gerry made her clean all the fish during the rest of their camping trip. But she'd learned her lesson even before that, thanks to that thunderstorm, and made a solemn promise never to hide from anyone again."

"Poor Aunt Jenna," Audrey said.

"Oh your dad got into trouble too."

Audrey's eyes widened. "He did? But he didn't do anything wrong."

"He was supposed to keep an eye on his little sister while they were fishing," Sarah explained, "but he was too busy trying to win the contest."

"What was his punishment?" Amy asked.

"Well, when they got back from their camping trip, Grandpa Gerry marched your dad down to the city manager's office and asked what Jason could do to help defray the cost of sending the search and rescue team up the mountain. The city manager told Jason he'd be in charge of picking up trash in the park for the rest of the summer."

"That sounds like a bigger punishment than Aunt Jenna got," Amy said. "That doesn't seem fair."

"Grandpa Gerry said that Jason was older and should have known better, that's why he got the harsher punishment." Gerry had been strict with the kids, but he always tried to be evenhanded.

Sarah wished he was here with her now.

A surge of power shot through the house and the lights came back on.

"Hooray," Audrey shouted, raising one fist in the air. "We've got the electricity back."

"Finally," Amy exclaimed, flopping back on the bed. Audrey flopped back too and they both started giggling.

Only Sarah didn't feel like joining them. The snow had stopped and the lights were back on—all good signs for leaving the inn.

There was only one thing missing—they still hadn't found Patrick. Until that happened, Sarah couldn't celebrate.

CHAPTER NINETEEN

Sarah paced back and forth in her room that evening, studying the notebook in her hands. Some of the guests had outright lied to her while others had withheld information that might reveal they had a motive to harm Patrick.

Then there was some of the strange behavior she had observed, such as Natalie's escape attempt that morning. She highlighted all the information in her notebook and sat back and reviewed it once more, hoping it might help point to the culprit.

Levi Prince – Hartford, CT. Employed by Patrick. Claims he drove to work Saturday morning and got caught in the blizzard. Has the only other key to the inn. Says backdoor was locked when he arrived. According to Finn, he was fired from his job the night of Patrick's disappearance. Served time in prison. Needs to be employed as a condition of his parole.

Finn Hawkins – New York, NY. Wanted to talk to Patrick in private the night before he disappeared. Now has a black eye. Was wearing the same suit from the night before when Dorothy's screams brought everyone to the parlor. According to Levi, Finn knew about the fire and safety code violations that could close down the inn. His lowball offer to buy the inn included a threat that Patrick would 'reap the consequences' if he refused to sell.

Dorothy Ogden – Schenectady, NY. Said Patrick told her she could use the kitchen to make tea. She found the mess in the parlor early Saturday morning. Worked in the banking industry before her retirement. Spent her honeymoon in the same room at this inn fifty years ago with her now deceased husband Leo. Heard the government inspector threaten to close down the inn.

Natalie Minnick – Concord, NH. Single mother with six-month-old baby. Bella cried for a good half hour during the night Patrick disappeared. Jobless. Claims she's staying here because she found a two-for-one coupon on the Red Clover Inn Web site. Tried to drive away from the inn this afternoon. Became hysterical. Keeps repeating that she made a mistake in coming here.

Chuck and Vonnie Thayer – Providence, RI. Married couple. Chuck was in a scuffle with Patrick the night he disappeared. Vonnie's mother used to own the inn and Vonnie lived here as a teen. She and Chuck sold the inn to Patrick ten years ago and recently offered to buy it back.

Patrick Maguire – Hartford, CT. Owner of the Red Clover Inn. Seemed to have problems with Levi, Finn, and Chuck the night of his disappearance. Keys and wallet still in his room. Behind on his bills. Paid bribes to the government inspector to keep the inn open until he ran out of money. Old baby photo in his wallet.

Then she added another name to the list:

Harvey Pittman – Inspector for the Connecticut Department of Public Safety. Found several fire and safety code violations at the inn. Took bribes to conceal the violations until Patrick ran out of money.

Sarah read through the data she'd collected. The answer was in there somewhere; she just needed to find it.

On the surface, it seemed that Finn and Levi had the most compelling motivations to harm Patrick. He controlled their livelihoods, in different ways. The government inspector was suspicious too, especially if Patrick had threatened to reveal the extortion scheme to the Connecticut Department of Public Safety.

Meanwhile, Levi and Finn were busy accusing each other of hurting Patrick while Vonnie was suspicious of Sarah herself.

She tossed the notebook onto the bed with a sigh of frustration and tangled her fingers in her hair. There was something she was missing. Something vital.

Sarah picked up the television remote and turned the TV on, needing a distraction.

"Our winter wonderland is almost over," the meteorologist said. "This slow-moving cold front is finally heading to the northeast and we can expect the temperatures to warm up to the high thirties or even low forties as early as tomorrow and for the rest of the week. ..."

That report didn't make her feel any better. Time was quickly running out. She switched off the television and walked over to the connecting door to peek inside the girls' room. She was relieved to see they were both sound asleep.

Her early weariness had vanished, replaced by a frenetic energy that made it difficult for her to stand still. Her cell phone lay on the dresser and she could see the red light blinking.

Martha had sent another cryptic text message: *Last chance.*

"What does that mean?" Sarah muttered and tried dialing Martha's number. The call still wouldn't go through, so she tried to send another text.

Last chance for what?

She pushed the send button and hoped her text message wouldn't bounce back this time. As soon as she returned to Maple Hill she was going to have a long talk with Martha. All these mysterious text messages were driving her batty.

Sarah set the cell phone back on the dresser and pulled open the drawer containing Maeve Maguire's Bible. After the day she'd just endured, she desperately needed some quiet time with God's word.

She turned the pages, looking at passages that Patrick's grandmother had marked with her pencil, until she found one in the second book of Corinthians that lifted her spirits and soothed her soul.

"Therefore we do not lose heart. Though outwardly we are wasting away, yet inwardly we are being renewed day by day. For our light and momentary troubles are achieving for us an eternal glory that far outweighs them all. So we fix our eyes not on what is seen, but on what is unseen. For what is seen is temporary, but what is unseen is eternal."

"Amen," Sarah said aloud, after reading the passage over again. Then she closed the Bible and placed it back in the drawer, feeling a little more at peace now.

She began to prepare for bed, changing into her nightgown and robe and washing her face at the bathroom sink. She ran a comb through her tousled, gray-blonde hair, the movement easing the tension in her temples and forehead.

Finally ready for bed, Sarah found herself humming the refrain of "In the Garden," one of her favorite hymns, as she pulled back the Grandmother's Puzzle quilt. She sat down on the side of the bed, smoothing one hand over the stitching on the underside of the quilt. Then she picked up one corner for a closer look, impressed by the tiny, even stitches in the creamy white quilt backing.

The quilt was at least a hundred years old but in so much better shape than the quilts in the attic. And it certainly smelled better.

The peace she had felt after reading Maeve's Bible vanished, replaced by the niggling thought that she was missing something important. Sarah kept thinking about those smelly quilts in the attic. The odor had been so strong, too strong for simple mold and mildew. She would need to investigate further if she ever wanted to get any sleep tonight.

Sarah walked to her bedroom door, peeking out into the hallway before closing her door and locking it behind her. She silently made her way to the attic. She knew she was breaking the rule she had set for herself and the girls, but she was running out of time. If she didn't find out what had happened to Patrick soon, she might never know.

Besides, she knew one scream would send everyone running to help. At least, that's what she told herself as she moved through the dark hallway.

Sarah climbed the attic stairs, wincing at the sound of aged wood squeaking under her feet. She remembered hearing someone else's footsteps up in the attic and wondered if others could hear her footsteps now. She opened the door and flipped on the light. This time she remembered exactly where the quilts were located and made a beeline for them.

She actually smelled them before she saw them, the acrid, tinny odor telling her that something definitely wasn't right. She had restored a lot of old quilts in her day and none of them had ever smelled quite like this.

Standing in front of the stack of old quilts, Sarah carefully lifted the top quilt off the pile. They were all tattered, but the one on the top looked different from the rest. When she held it toward the light, she could see why.

It was covered with red.

The stains had soaked through all three layers of the quilt, turning many of the light fabrics a dirty brown color. She could still make out the quilt pattern though. It was a Wedding Ring quilt. She had suspected that someone had covered Patrick's wounds with a blanket of some sort and this quilt might prove it. She held it up to her nose, inhaling a strong metallic odor. It could be blood, but the fabric wasn't stiff to the touch like it would be if blood had dried there.

Sarah stepped back, holding the quilt in front of her. Then she carefully fingered one of the stains, powdery rust coming off on her skin. It wasn't blood at all.

Realization dawned on her when she looked up at the rafters. Someone had nailed pieces of aluminum flashing along the peak, most of it now covered with rust. Levi had blamed the chandelier crash on a leaky roof. It obviously leaked in more than one place. Patrick must have opted for a cheap repair that hadn't fixed the problem at all.

She studied the floor around the pile of quilts, finding evidence of old rusty water stains there too. With a sigh of disappointment, she folded the damaged quilt and placed it back on the pile.

The worst part was that she'd been so sure. Something had told her these quilts were the key. Only now she was walking away empty-handed. She checked the rest of the quilts, just to be sure there wasn't a bloody one hidden among them but no luck.

A few had some water and rust damage, but none were as bad as the quilt on the top of the pile. As a vintage quilt restorer, it saddened her to see these quilts in such bad shape. Any other time, she would have taken them downstairs with her and started figuring out how to restore them, but at this moment she just didn't have the drive. Not when Patrick was still missing and she had failed in her quest to find him.

She headed toward the attic door, the odor of rusty fabric still lingering in her nostrils. As she descended the stairs, she could hear Bella crying. All the bedroom doors were closed though and no one appeared as Sarah made her way back to her room.

When she opened the door, she heard a gasp of surprise and saw someone standing near her dresser, arms buried elbow-deep in the middle drawer.

"Dorothy!" Sarah cried. "What do you think you're doing?"

CHAPTER TWENTY

Sarah strode into her bedroom. "Dorothy? What are you doing?"

But she could see perfectly well what Dorothy was doing. All the dresser drawers were pulled open and half the contents had spilled out, including Maeve's Bible, which lay open, face down, on the wood floor.

Sarah leaned down to pick it up, smoothing the bent pages. She couldn't believe Dorothy would do something like this.

"It's not what it looks like," Dorothy said, her face pale. She hurried toward the open door, but instead of making a run for it, Dorothy closed the door and turned around to face Sarah.

"Not what it looks like?" Sarah repeated, noting that Dorothy no longer wore the polished suit she'd had on earlier today. She was dressed in a black sweatshirt and matching pants, her hair pulled back into a tight bun. "It looks like you're rifling through my things. Is this what happened to Patrick? Did he catch you trying to steal from him too?"

Indignation flashed in her green eyes. "I am not trying to steal from anybody!"

Sarah took a deep breath, trying to figure out why Dorothy was acting so offended. "If you're not trying to steal from me, then how did you get in my room?"

Dorothy's eyes shifted. "The door was open."

"No, it wasn't," Sarah said firmly. She'd made certain both of the bedroom doors were locked before going up to the attic, not wanting to give anyone access to her sleeping granddaughters.

Dorothy sighed. "What does it matter how I got in? You caught me in your room. I need to know what you're going to do about it."

Good question.

Sarah walked to the bed and sat down, wondering if Dorothy had made a habit of rifling through everyone's belongings. If so, how had she gotten in?

"I should call everyone in here," Sarah said at last, "and tell them I caught you red-handed going through all my things."

"I'll just tell them the truth—that I was looking for evidence that you're the one who hurt Patrick."

Sarah blinked. "You're accusing me of hurting Patrick?"

"You had the cellar key, didn't you? I think the police will be quite interested in that fact. Along with some other things I've discovered."

"What things?"

Dorothy shook her head. "I know better than to show you my hand."

"You're missing one crucial element: motive. I've never even met Patrick before. Why would I want to hurt him?"

Before Dorothy could reply, a sleepy Amy appeared in the doorway between the two rooms. Her blonde braids hung crookedly on her shoulders, half the hair hanging out of the weave. She squinted at the light. "What's going on?"

"Nothing, dear," Sarah said, walking over to her. "Go on back to bed."

"Can I have a drink of water first?"

"Yes, I'll get one for you." Sarah escorted Amy back to bed before going into the bathroom to fill a glass with water. When she took it to Amy, her granddaughter took a few sips and set it on the table beside her.

"Thanks, Grandma."

"You're welcome, dear." Sarah walked back into her room, closing the connecting door far enough to keep the light from seeping into the girls' room. Then she turned around to confront Dorothy about her ridiculous accusations.

Only Dorothy wasn't there.

Sarah walked to her door and opened it, but the hallway was empty. Either Dorothy had gone back to her room or was continuing her search for evidence to prove Sarah guilty.

In her heart of hearts, she couldn't really blame the woman. The fact that she'd suddenly found the cellar key probably had looked suspicious. And wasn't Dorothy doing the same thing as Sarah—trying to find out what had happened to Patrick?

Only Sarah didn't break into people's rooms to find clues—a fact that still bothered her. She walked over to the dresser, wondering if she could shove it against the door herself or if she'd need help. With half the drawers' contents on the floor, it moved pretty easily. She removed the largest of the drawers and started pushing it toward the door.

She'd have to do the same thing in the girls' room if she wanted to get any sleep tonight. At this point, Sarah didn't trust Dorothy or anyone else in this house.

A wounded cry sounded from the hallway.

"Not again," Sarah murmured, rushing to her door. She stepped out into the hall, and as she turned to lock the door behind her, Vonnie and Chuck hurried past her toward Dorothy's room. She followed them and gasped when she saw the elderly woman crumpled in her open doorway.

"What happened?" Sarah asked as Levi and Finn emerged from their rooms. She noticed that Dorothy had changed out of her black sweat suit and into her nightgown and robe.

"I don't know." Vonnie knelt down beside the woman and slowly tipped up Dorothy's chin with one finger.

That's when Sarah saw the ugly red gash on Dorothy's forehead.

"She's hurt," Vonnie said, holding a hand out toward Chuck. "Give me your handkerchief."

Chuck pulled a clean white handkerchief from his shirt pocket and handed it to his wife. "How did she hurt herself? Did she fall?"

"I don't know yet," Vonnie said as she gently dabbed the wound.

Dorothy's eyelids fluttered and a low moan sounded in her throat.

Finn stepped forward, looking up and down the hallway. "Did anyone see what happened?"

"I just heard her cry out," Sarah replied, noticing that Natalie hadn't appeared yet. The noise obviously hadn't awakened the twins or they'd be out in the hallway with her.

Dorothy moaned again, louder this time, right before she opened her eyes. "Where am I?"

Blood from the angry wound on her forehead had dripped down her face and onto her terry cloth robe, staining the white lace collar. She was barefoot, her toes swollen and twisted by arthritis.

This woman looked so frail and vulnerable compared to the one Sarah had caught in her room just a short while ago. When Dorothy's fingers moved toward the wound, Sarah knelt down and took her hand to keep her from touching it.

"There now," Vonnie said, holding the handkerchief to the bleeding wound. "It's not as bad as it looks. Head wounds always bleed a lot."

"Can you tell us what happened?" Chuck asked Dorothy.

Shadows clouded the older woman's face as she looked up at the people surrounding her. "I'm not sure. I opened my door to go downstairs and fix myself a cup of tea. I thought it would be safe with everyone in bed. Then someone suddenly rushed past me and pushed me down."

"Who was it?" Vonnie asked her.

Dorothy's eyes fluttered. "Sarah."

"She's right here, holding your hand," Vonnie assured her, gently dabbing at the wound on Dorothy's forehead.

"No," Dorothy whispered. "Sarah's the one who did this to me."

Levi's eyes widened in shock. "Sarah?"

Sarah reflexively let go of the woman's hand and leaned away from her, horrified by the accusation. "That's not true. I was in my room."

"You were out in the hallway when I saw you," Chuck said. "Closer to Dorothy than anyone else.

"She's making it up," Sarah said. "In fact, I caught Dorothy going through my dresser drawers when I came back from…" Sarah's voice trailed off when she realized that her trip to the attic would only make her look more suspicious.

People had complained about hearing the creak of footsteps above them the night before. If Sarah admitted to an unauthorized trip to the attic tonight, they might think her guilty of wandering around and believe Dorothy's lie that Sarah had attacked her.

"Making it up?" Finn scoffed. "That blood on her head looks pretty real to me."

"It's real," Vonnie said curtly, still dabbing at the wound. "How could anyone do something like this to an old woman?"

Sarah looked at the people gathered around her. From the expressions on their faces, they already had doubts about her. Why would they believe anything Sarah said about Dorothy now?

Maybe Dorothy had assumed it was Sarah who pushed her down, especially after their confrontation in Sarah's room. The hallway was dim and Dorothy's description of someone rushing past her made it probable that she hadn't gotten a clear look at her assailant's face.

"I don't care what it looks like, it wasn't me," Sarah reiterated and turned to Dorothy. "Which way was this person going?" she asked, "toward the stairs or down the hallway?"

Dorothy sighed. "I don't know. I didn't actually see my attacker, but I know it was intentional. I was putting clues together and finally thought I had an answer—"

"What are you saying?" Vonnie asked, glancing at Sarah. "Do you know who hurt Patrick?"

Sarah held her breath, waiting for the older woman to accuse her of that too.

"No," Dorothy said at last. She squeezed her eyes shut as she tested the depth of the wound. "Now I can't remember anything."

Finn sighed. "So you really don't know if Sarah's the one who knocked you down. She's just the first one you saw in the hallway. Is that right?"

"I don't know," Dorothy said weakly. "I'm so confused."

"I don't think she'll need stitches," Vonnie said. "I'll put a butterfly bandage on it for now and a doctor can take a look at it tomorrow."

"I wish I could go tonight." Dorothy looked imploringly at Levi. "Is there any way I can get to a hospital? Would Patrick's truck make it through the drifts?"

Levi shook his head. "I'm sorry, Dorothy. They're just too high."

"It's better if you're not bouncing around in a truck anyway," Vonnie said. "You might have a concussion."

Natalie's door cracked open and she peeked her head outside. "What's going on?"

"Dorothy got hurt," Levi moved toward her door, "but it looks like she's going to be all right."

Natalie stepped out of her room, closing the door softly behind her. She wore a pair of yellow pajama pants topped with a thin thermal undershirt. "How did it happen?"

Levi repeated the story Dorothy had told them.

Dorothy reached a hand toward Chuck. "Will you please help me up?"

Chuck glanced at his wife, who nodded her approval. Then he grasped Dorothy's thin arms and carefully lifted her to her feet. He held on until she'd steadied herself.

"I'm all right," she said and she smoothed down the front of her robe. "Embarrassed, but okay."

"There's no reason to be embarrassed." Vonnie gave the bloody handkerchief back to her husband. "Does your head hurt anywhere else?"

Dorothy hesitated a moment. "No. It's sore, but I don't have a headache, if that's what you mean."

"How about anywhere else?" Vonnie reached out and felt her arms and ribs. "Any sore spots here?"

Dorothy shook her head.

"I think you'll be fine," Vonnie replied. "It still wouldn't hurt for me to check on you tonight, if you don't mind. I could use your extra key to let myself in."

"Of course," Dorothy said, turning toward her room.

"Are you sure that's safe?" Natalie asked.

Vonnie spun around. "Do you really think I'd hurt someone like Dorothy? I've spent the last ten years taking care of the elderly."

"Someone just knocked her down. And it was one of us."

Vonnie sniffed. "Well, I'd hardly offer to help in front of everyone if I planned on hurting her, would I?"

Natalie shrank from Vonnie's harsh words. "I guess not."

A tremulous smile curved Dorothy's mouth. "I'm not afraid of you, Vonnie. You wait right here while I go get that spare key."

"So now what do we do?" Levi asked.

Finn turned toward his room. "Go back to bed, unless you have a better idea."

"Maybe someone should stand watch in the hallway," Chuck suggested, glancing at Sarah. "Just to be safe."

His words sent a chill through her. He meant safe from her.

Finn shook his head. "I think we should all just go back in our rooms and lock our doors. As far as I'm concerned, the sooner we get out of this place, the safer we'll all be."

Dorothy returned to the hallway and handed Vonnie her spare key. "Don't feel you have to check on me if you think it's not safe."

"Nonsense," Vonnie told her. "You're just one door down and everybody will hear me if I scream."

"That's right," Dorothy said, her gaze moving to Sarah. "One scream and they'll all come running."

The irony of that statement hit Sarah full force. When she had climbed the stairs to the attic, she had thought almost exactly the same thing to reassure herself that she would be safe.

Now she was the one they were afraid of.

CHAPTER TWENTY-ONE

"Hold on there, Sarah," Vonnie called after her. Sarah stood at her door, her hand on the knob as Vonnie and Chuck approached her. "What?"

"I think it's time we're straight with each other," Vonnie told her.

Well, that would be a nice change. Vonnie and Chuck had told so many lies she could barely keep them straight. "What do you mean?"

"Chuck and I know why you came here this weekend and it wasn't for any quilting conference."

"Then why do you think I'm here?"

"For the money," Chuck blurted out.

The money?

Vonnie took a step closer to her. "Don't play coy with us. You've found it already, haven't you."

It dawned on Sarah that she was being presented with a brand-new reason for Patrick's disappearance, and she needed to keep Chuck and Vonnie talking so she could glean more information. "What makes you think I've already found it?"

"You've dropped the devoted grandmother act. Attacking Dorothy? Desperate move."

"I didn't..." She let her words trail off, forcing herself to play along. "I don't know what you're talking about."

"Fine. If that's how you're going to play the game. It belongs to me anyway. To my mother, actually. We're just trying to find what's rightfully ours."

"I don't believe her," Chuck said bluntly. "Sarah has it."

"How would I have it? I've never heard of it before."

"But you just said—"

"I said nothing. I just let you talk."

Vonnie was speechless. Sarah knew she had to keep her talking.

"Why didn't your mother take the money with her when she sold you the inn?"

Vonnie folded her arms across her chest. "She didn't actually sell the inn to us. Chuck and I took it over when we finally realized she was experiencing memory loss. By then, she didn't remember where she'd hidden it."

Sarah knew how hard it was to see a parent lose his memories. Her father had lucid moments, but he was often confused. At least he was happy most of the time. For that, she was thankful.

"Come on, Vonnie," Chuck said. "Let's go."

"My mother was very good at hiding things." A look of frustration passed over her face. "She said she put it in a basket to save for a rainy day."

"It's raining, is it?"

"Cats and dogs," Chuck mumbled. "Nursing bills, mortgage...."

"Mother started a new medication a few months ago," Vonnie continued. "It's really helped her memory a lot."

"She remembers the money again?"

Vonnie replied. "Chuck and I are here to claim what is rightfully ours."

Sarah knew there was more to the story. "You believe the inn is yours too, don't you?"

Vonnie blanched. "What do you mean?"

"I discovered some legal documents among Patrick's papers. He bought this inn when it was in foreclosure. I assume you and Chuck were about to lose it."

Vonnie's mouth tightened. "Times were tight then. Chuck had just had his first knee surgery and I was busy taking care of him. We let things go here a little and our business began to suffer. We could have rebounded, though, if Patrick Maguire hadn't come along and stolen the inn out from under us."

The Thayers had just catapulted to the top of Sarah's suspect list. Not only were they searching for hidden money, but they believed Patrick had robbed them of their beloved home and livelihood. What better motive for making him disappear? But Sarah sensed she still wasn't getting the full story from the Thayers. Why would Vonnie's mother hide money at the inn? Why not put it in a bank? She knew some people from that generation often had a mistrust of banks—her own grandfather had been one of them. They'd gone through the Great Depression and seen too many banks fail to feel safe keeping their money in one.

But that might not be the only reason Paulette Remmer had decided to hide money in the inn instead of depositing it in the local bank.

"Let's go, Vonnie," Chuck said, grabbing her arm. Turning to Sarah, he said, "Stay out of our way. Leave the money to us. If you don't, we'll back up Dorothy's charges of assault when the police arrive."

"But you didn't see anything."

"They won't know that."

"Finn and Levi will back me up," she said, hoping it was true. "At the very least, they know neither one of you said anything just now about seeing me hit Dorothy."

Chuck scoffed. "Finn's in such a big hurry to get back to New York that I doubt he'll stick around long enough to give a statement. And Levi's an ex-con. Who's going to believe him?"

Sarah suddenly realized she didn't feel safe alone with the Thayers in the hallway. They were already threatening to file a false police report to keep her from finding their precious money. What else might they do?

"I'm going to bed now," Sarah said, opening her door.

Chuck nodded. "Sleep on it. I'm sure you'll see things our way in the morning."

She watched them walk away and disappear into their room. Then she slipped inside her own room and locked the door, her hands shaking.

To her surprise, the twins still slept soundly in the other room. She checked the lock on their door, making sure it was secure and wedged a chair in front of it to prevent anyone from entering unannounced.

Walking back into her own room, Sarah heard a light tapping sound on her door.

Her first thought was that Chuck and Vonnie had come back to threaten her some more. Then she heard Natalie's reed-thin voice through the wood.

"Sarah, are you there? I need your help."

Sarah opened the door and saw raw fear etched on Natalie's young face.

"Something's wrong with Bella," Natalie cried.

Sarah didn't wait for an explanation. She hurried down the hallway to Natalie's room.

"I didn't know what to do," Natalie said as she quickly led Sarah into her room. "I thought since you're a mother and a grandmother you might be able to figure out what's wrong with her."

Bella sat up in her crib, her eyes red rimmed and her nose running. Her breathing was heavy and labored, punctuated by a deep, chest-rattling cough.

Sarah recognized that cough. It was the same one that had tormented Jason for the first three years of his life.

"It's croup," Sarah said, gathering up the baby in her arms. She picked up the crib blanket and wrapped it around her and placed her cheek against Bella's forehead. "I think she has a fever too."

Levi suddenly appeared in the doorway, hastily pulling on a gray flannel shirt over the white T-shirt he wore. "What's going on?"

Natalie turned around. "Bella is sick. We've got to find a way to get out of here and get her to a doctor."

Levi met Sarah's gaze and he looked back at Natalie. "I'm sorry, the roads still aren't clear. And the phone line is still down, so there's no way to call for help."

Bella started coughing again, sounding completely miserable. Sarah carried her to the door. "We've got to take her outside."

"What?" Natalie followed her into the hallway and down the stairs. "You said she has a fever. If we take her out in this cold, she'll catch pneumonia!"

"We won't keep her out there long," Sarah promised, hurrying down the steps and moving toward the kitchen with the baby in her arms.

"Are you sure you know what you're doing?" Levi asked, keeping pace with Natalie.

Sarah headed for the screened porch. "I've done it a few times before—when my son was a baby." She didn't blame them for doubting her. It didn't make sense to take a sick baby out into the cold air, even if it did work.

What really surprised her was that Natalie had come to her at all after Dorothy's accusation. Maybe that's why Levi had suddenly appeared at the door—as a bodyguard for Natalie and Bella.

Whatever the reason, she was glad to see Natalie and Levi talking again.

When they reached the screened porch, the cool air startled Bella. She even stopped crying and looked around as Sarah wrapped the baby blanket more snugly around her.

"Brrr," Natalie said as she stepped onto the all-weather carpet. "It's so cold out here."

Levi took off his flannel shirt and handed it to Natalie. "Here. Put this on."

Natalie hesitated. "But you're only wearing a T-shirt. You'll freeze."

"I'm plenty warm," Levi insisted.

Sarah smiled to herself as she turned her attention back to the baby. Another cough rattled Bella's chest, making Sarah wince. She hoped this method worked the way it had with Jason, otherwise it was going to be a very long night.

After a few minutes, Bella's labored breathing began to ease.

"Am I just imagining it," Natalie asked in amazement, "or does she sound better?"

Sarah nodded. "She does. The cold air shrinks the swelling in her windpipe. We'll stay out here another minute or two and then take her back up to your room. The next best thing for croup is warm, moist air. You can turn on your shower and get the bathroom nice and steamy."

Natalie stared at Sarah. "Will I ever know as much about children as you?"

"You'll learn as you go, just like every other mother. I've had lots of years to practice." She sighed. "Too many to count, in fact."

"I hope you're right." Natalie looked thoughtful. "I just don't want to screw it up."

"You won't," Levi told her. "You seem like a great mom to me."

Natalie blushed. "Thanks. I'm working on it."

Sarah was relieved that the cold air treatment had worked so well. The baby's cough had lessened and her breathing wasn't as labored. When they headed back into the house, Bella started squirming a bit. "Do you want your mommy now?"

Bella gurgled and held out her arms to Natalie. Sarah handed over the baby to her. "Here you go."

"Isabella Hope," Natalie said firmly, "don't you ever scare me like that again." Then she gathered the baby in her arms and held her close.

A tingle of recognition prompted Sarah to ask, "Hope?"

"Hope was my mom's name."

Sarah stared at her, remembering the lace christening gown she'd seen in Natalie's photo. The same lace pattern as the curtains in her room. There was that other baby photo too, the one Patrick had kept in his wallet all these years.

"Natalie, are you Patrick's daughter?" Sarah asked her.

Natalie stared at her. "How did you know?"

"Your mother's name is in the Maguire family Bible," Sarah told her. "And I recognized the lace pattern of Bella's christening gown. It was made by her great-great-grandmother, wasn't it?"

Natalie nodded. "I never met her, but that's what my mom told me. She gave it to mom just before I was born."

Levi's mouth gaped. "Patrick never told me he had a daughter."

"That's because he doesn't know," Natalie replied. "I mean, he knows he has a daughter, but he doesn't know it's me. I didn't tell him I was coming."

Sarah stood back, certain she would learn more by listening to their conversation then by asking questions of her own. She had known there had to be a good reason a young girl in Natalie's financial straits would choose to stay at an out-of-the-way place like the Red Clover Inn.

"How is that possible?" Levi asked. "He knows your name, doesn't he?"

"I guess not." Disappointment seeped into her voice. "I never knew Patrick. He and my mom divorced shortly after I was born. She sent him pictures of me for a while, but then she met my stepdad and they got married. He died about three years ago."

Sarah wondered what it was like for Natalie to grow up never knowing her biological father. She had recently lost her mother and stepfather and now, mysteriously, Patrick was lost to her too.

"Why did you decide to meet him now?" Sarah asked, finally breaking her silence.

Natalie turned to her. "I don't know. Just curious, I guess."

That answer didn't ring true. After nineteen years, something had to have prompted the girl to seek him out. "I'm guessing there's no day care job waiting for you in Hartford, is there?"

Natalie hesitated. "No."

"So you came here for the sole reason of meeting Patrick," Sarah continued, still trying to work it out in her head, "yet you didn't introduce yourself when you got here."

Anger flared in Natalie's brown eyes. "Yes, is that so wrong? He pretended I didn't exist for nineteen years. Nineteen years! I'm his daughter. I'm supposed to matter."

Sarah could hear the pain in her voice. Patrick hadn't even written Natalie's name and birth date in his grandmother's Bible. She hoped there was a reason other than just not caring enough to do it.

Bella began to fuss in Natalie's arms, frightened by the sudden change in her mother's tone. Natalie instantly wilted and leaned down to console her child.

"It's all right, Bella. Mommy's here. I won't ever leave you."

Sarah sensed that Natalie didn't know what she was feeling. The girl had said more than once that she wished she'd never come here. Perhaps she'd been imagining a tearful reunion with her birth father and been bitterly disappointed.

But bitter enough to hurt him?

There was another element to consider too, a purely financial one. If Patrick disappeared, Natalie, as his direct heir, could claim ownership to the Red Clover Inn. It was worth something, even with the safety code violations. Natalie could sell it and have a nice little nest egg for herself and her daughter.

"I'd better take her upstairs," Natalie said, "and start the shower. I don't want her to start coughing like that again."

Sarah followed her out of the kitchen with Levi close behind them. He still seemed stunned by the news of Natalie's paternity.

"You'll want to let her breathe the steamy air for about ten minutes," Sarah told her as they mounted the stairs. "Then you should be able to lay her down to sleep. Just let me know if you need any help."

"Thank you." Natalie stopped at her door, her gaze moving to Levi. "You probably want your shirt back."

"That's okay." He cleared his throat. "You can give it to me tomorrow."

Natalie nodded and disappeared into her room with Bella. Sarah heard the lock turn on the door and looked at Levi. "So you didn't know Patrick had a daughter?"

He shook his head. "No. I never even knew he'd been married." He met her gaze. "Why would he keep a secret like that?"

Sarah supposed there were a lot of reasons. Talking about a daughter he'd never known might be too painful for him. Or perhaps he'd made himself forget—even going so far as to keep her name out of the family Bible.

Sarah returned to her room, fatigue finally setting in.

She checked on the sleeping twins once more and climbed into her bed with a sigh of relief. A full moon shone through the window, illuminating the portrait of Patrick's grandmother on the wall. Sarah imagined she could see a resemblance to Natalie.

Had Patrick really not recognized his own daughter or had he been waiting for her to make the first move? Sarah pulled the quilt up around her shoulders as she settled into the pillow. Thinking about Patrick and Natalie made her miss her own father. William Drayton had never made Sarah doubt his love for her.

She closed her eyes, knowing her Heavenly Father was always with her. That thought comforted her as she breathed a silent prayer for her family and friends in Maple Hill.

Then she prayed for Natalie and Bella and Levi, as well as the rest of the guests at the inn, including Dorothy and the

Thayers. They all faced problems, but someone had gone too far when they'd assaulted Patrick.

And if she ever figured out who that person was, they would have a lot more to worry about.

CHAPTER TWENTY-TWO

Before dawn the next morning, Sarah awoke to a light, steady tapping on her bedroom door. "Who is it?" she groaned, exhausted from late nights and early morning wake-up calls. She felt as if she hadn't slept at all.

No one answered.

Sarah leaned up on one elbow. "Who's there?"

Still no answer.

Worried that Bella might be having trouble with the croup again, Sarah climbed out of bed and donned her flannel robe and thick, wool slippers. She cinched the robe snugly around her waist as she made her way across the room.

She slowly opened the door but no one was on the other side. On the floor in front of her was a typewritten note. She stooped down to pick it up and read the short, two-sentence missive.

Your detective licence has finally expired. Stop this investigation or you and your granddaughters will reap the consequences.

A cold chill washed over her that had nothing to do with the wintry weather outside. "Reap the consequences" was the same phrase Finn had used in his letter. Had he left this at her door or had it been left by someone who wanted her to suspect him?

Sarah started to read the threatening lines again, then heard the sound of footsteps on the stairs. She hurried down the hallway, determined to see who had left such a nasty note at her door. Practically running down the stairs, Sarah stumbled when one of her slippers slid on a step.

She steadied herself before continuing her chase, growing more and more angry that someone would even hint at harming her sweet granddaughters.

When she reached the landing at the bottom of the staircase, she saw the front door standing wide open. A cold wind blew through the front foyer and swirled around her. She moved quickly to close the door but saw a strange, glowing light to the right of the house, near the driveway. It was low to the ground and Sarah couldn't see the source.

The sun hadn't come up yet, so she couldn't tell if anyone was hiding out there behind one of the cars. With the electricity working again, Levi would have no reason to go outside this early in the morning and neither would anyone else.

So what was the light?

She stuck the letter into the deep pocket of her robe and stepped outside on the front porch for a closer look. A scant moment later, the front door slammed closed behind her and she heard the sickening sound of the dead bolt locking into place.

Sarah realized too late that she'd just walked into a frozen trap. She turned around and pounded on the solid oak door, even though she knew it was a wasted effort. Someone had lured her out here, but why?

Because she was getting too close to the truth?

The reason wouldn't matter if she froze to death. She stepped off the porch and headed for the light. Fortunately, the moon's reflection off the snow provided enough light for her to see in the dark. Cold, wet snow dropped into her slippers as she waded through the drifts, making it difficult to keep the footwear on.

When she finally reached the driveway, she saw a flashlight in the snow. Clearly she had walked into a trap. Sarah looked up at the inn. There were no lights shining in the second floor windows, which meant everyone was still asleep.

Everyone but the miscreant who had locked her out of the inn. Perhaps he or she had already gone back to bed, considering the problem neatly solved.

Only Sarah wasn't ready to give up that easily.

"Help me!" she shouted, moving closer to the inn. "Someone please help me!" The howling wind muffled her voice and made it impossible for anyone to hear her.

She knew hypothermia could set in within minutes, so she didn't have a second to lose. Sarah hurried over to the house and started digging through the piles of snow, hoping to find landscaping rocks or something hard she could throw at the second floor windows.

Her nose started to run and her bare fingers grew numb. She could barely feel her feet as she walked. With a grunt of frustration, Sarah gave up looking for rocks. She had to find some other way back into the house.

She hastily looked all around her, seeing portions of the three different cellar windows she had uncovered while searching for rocks. She pushed more snow away to reveal the full window in the center, but knew without a doubt that she would never fit through it.

She had to find another way.

Gasping for breath, Sarah stood in the snow facing the house. That's when she noticed something odd.

The cellar windows.

There were three of them. But how was that possible when she had seen only two windows from inside the cellar on Saturday? If there was a third window, that meant there was a wall that she hadn't seen. A room in the cellar she hadn't seen.

A secret room. She knew where to find Patrick.

Sarah hurried toward the shed, feeling exhilarated that she had finally put the right clues together. But despite her newfound energy, her body felt like it was moving in slow motion. Thanks to Gerry's expertise in survival skills, she knew how to recognize the symptoms of hypo-thermia.

First, shivering and feeling weak. Then, stumbling and mild confusion, followed by difficulty speaking and irra-tional behavior. Some people experiencing severe symp-toms of hypothermia even started taking off their clothes because the part of their brain regulating body temperature no longer functioned properly.

Gerry had taught her well during their many camping trips. She again wished he was here to help her now, but Sarah had to figure this out on her own. She was already shivering and her body felt sluggish. The desire to lie down on a snow drift and fall asleep was almost overwhelming.

But she pushed on, determined to rescue Patrick. Be-sides, stopping now would be too dangerous.

When Sarah reached the shed, she got a short respite from the cold wind. But the frozen water in a bucket near the tile saw was proof that the shed wasn't a safe place for her either. She was out of the wind but still exposed to freez-ing temperatures. She realized trying to wake someone to help her would take too long. She needed to find somewhere warm. Now.

She walked over to the shed's window, wiping the grimy film off the glass so she could see outside. Her breath came out in puffs of frosty air and her mind felt slightly fuzzy. It took her a moment to realize that the answer lay right in front of her.

The screened porch.

The porch door was locked, but all she had to do was break through one of the mesh screens and she'd be able to get back inside the warm house.

Sarah looked around the shed for something to break through the screen. She saw a steel snow shovel hanging high from a rusty nail. Reaching out to grab the blade, Sarah's hand faltered a little, the edge of the steel cutting her as she lifted the shovel off the nail. Sarah saw a ribbon of blood on her palm between her thumb and forefinger, but she didn't feel any pain.

Not a good sign.

She squared her shoulders and headed back outside, the wind striking her as soon as she stepped through the shed door. Sarah lowered her head as she made her way through the portico to the screened porch. The shovel felt so heavy as she dragged it behind her and Sarah feared she might be losing what little strength she had left.

It seemed like hours before she finally reached the porch. She stopped for a moment to catch her breath, wondering if she should sit down to rest for a while.

Last chance.

The words echoed in her head and for a moment she couldn't remember where she had heard them before. Martha's text. She had sent Sarah that message last night and now it resonated with her in a way Martha certainly hadn't meant.

There were people counting on her. Martha and the twins and Jason and Maggie. Jenna and David and Thomas and Jonathan. Her father and her friends at Bridge Street Church.

Patrick most urgently of all.

Thinking of them gave Sarah the strength she needed to go on. She lifted the shovel and swung it against the mesh screen. The blade bounced harmlessly against it and fell back into the snow.

"Please help me, Lord," Sarah prayed aloud, thankful that she could still speak. That meant she hadn't reached the more serious stages of hypothermia yet. As long as she could still walk and talk, she had a chance.

She picked up the shovel again and swung it like a baseball bat at the screen. The tip of the shovel made a tiny hole in the mesh, barely big enough for a mosquito to crawl through, much less a grown woman.

But it was a start.

Sarah swung again and again, each time making the hole just a little bit bigger. She lost count of the number of times she hit the shovel against the screen, her arms aching at the effort. She was thankful she could still feel them. The exercise did help get her blood pumping, helping to counteract the frigid air that threatened to numb her from head to toe.

As the hole in the screen grew bigger, the shovel blade did more damage, ripping a wider opening each time she swung. At last, Sarah believed the hole was big enough for her to crawl through. She dropped the shovel and battled to hoist one cold, stiff leg over the wooden ledge and through the screen.

It took three tries, but she finally pushed through. She balanced on the narrow ledge for a moment and swung her other leg over. The momentum caused her to tumble onto the all-weather carpet.

Sarah breathed a prayer of thanks as she struggled to rise to her feet. Her limbs were stiff from cold and she found it difficult to lift herself off the floor. She grabbed onto the ledge beside her and used it to propel herself onto her knees. Then she pulled herself up the rest of the way.

To her surprise, the crocheted slippers were still on her feet. Snow clung to the yarn, but they'd protected her bare feet from the worst of it.

She stumbled toward the kitchen door, holding onto the wooden ledge for support. Then she turned the cold brass doorknob and walked inside the kitchen. The heat from the kitchen wrapped around her like a warm blanket.

Sarah knew she needed to take care of her frozen hands and feet before she did anything else. She made it to a chair near the stove and collapsed on it, feeling as if every bit of energy had been drained from her body.

After resting for several moments, she twisted the oven dial on the electric stove and opened the oven door, letting the heat wash over her body.

She removed the crocheted slippers and held her feet and hands close to the hot oven, biting her lip as a painful pins and needles sensation started crawling over her skin. Despite the pain, Sarah knew that was a good sign—her circulation was getting back to normal.

When she had recovered enough to stand, she put the teakettle on the stove, waiting impatiently for the water to boil. It took all her willpower to stay in the kitchen instead of shouting her news to the rest of the guests, but she needed all her strength for what lay ahead of her.

As she sat back down in the chair, Sarah realized how close she had come to freezing out there.

"Thank you, Lord, for watching out for me," Sarah said aloud, her heart pounding from her close call. "Thank you for giving me the strength to keep going."

She had no idea how long she had been outside. It had seemed like forever, but she knew it couldn't have been more then fifteen or twenty minutes. She wouldn't have survived the bitter cold longer than that, especially wearing only a robe over her nightgown and slippers.

When the teakettle began to whistle, Sarah stood up and made herself a cup of tea. She added a good dollop of honey, knowing she could use the energy it would provide. Then she took a cautious sip of the hot brew.

The tea warmed her from the inside out and Sarah started to feel more like herself. As she sipped her tea, she thought about everything that had happened since she had heard the strange tapping at her door this morning.

She stood up, almost spilling the small amount of tea left in her cup and made her way out of the kitchen and up the stairs, moving as fast as she could on her half-frozen feet. As she walked down the second floor hallway she knocked on each and every door.

Chuck stuck his head out into the hallway, his beefy cheeks half-covered with shaving cream. "What's going on out here?"

Natalie walked out of her room fully dressed in a red V-neck sweater and blue jeans, a sniffling Bella in her arms. "What's wrong?"

"Everyone needs to meet me down in the parlor right away."

"What for?" Finn asked, raking a hand over his unruly dark hair.

"I'll tell you when we get there." Sarah hurried into her room and moved through the connecting doorway to awaken the girls.

"Amy!" she whispered loudly, gently shaking her granddaughter's shoulder. "Audrey! You two need to get up right now." She leaned over the bed to shake Audrey awake. "Come on, girls, please wake up."

Amy squinted up at Sarah. "What time is it?"

Sarah glanced at the pine timber clock on the bedside table. "Almost seven o'clock."

"In the morning?" Audrey groaned as she turned over to face Sarah. "Why do we have to get up so early?"

"Because I know where to find Patrick."

CHAPTER TWENTY-THREE

inn and Levi arrived in the parlor first, both of them bleary-eyed. Levi wore a T-shirt and jeans, not bothering to hide the prison tattoo peeking beneath his short sleeve.

A shadow of whiskers covered Finn's face and the wrinkled tail of his white dress shirt hung out the back of his gray slacks.

The Thayers and Dorothy followed soon after. Chuck and Vonnie were fully dressed in matching red and white warm-up suits and white tennis shoes. A wad of tissue paper was stuck to Chuck's chin where he'd cut himself shaving. Vonnie's salt-and-pepper curls were pulled back into a loose ponytail.

They supported Dorothy between them. She was still wearing her blood-stained robe, and the red gash stood out on her pale temple, made all the more prominent by the fact that she had combed her hair off her forehead.

That told Sarah all she needed to know about the woman's intentions.

Natalie and Bella arrived last, the wide-eyed daughter looking much more alert than her sleepy mother. Natalie had Bella in flannel, one-piece pajamas that zipped up the front. The baby sniffled, rubbing her nose against her mother's shoulder.

"Now that we're all here," Finn said, "do you want to tell us what's going on?"

"I'm assuming at least one of you isn't happy to see me here," Sarah said, observing their reactions to her statement. Most of them appeared confused rather than guilty.

"Someone locked me out of the inn this morning," Sarah explained.

"What?" Natalie exclaimed. "In this weather?"

Sarah nodded as the twins huddled close to her. She put her arms around them, grateful for the warmth they gave her, both inside and out. "Fortunately, I was able to break in through the screened porch and get back inside, but it was a very close call."

"Are you all right, Grandma?" Amy asked, worry straining her voice.

"I'm fine," she assured both of the girls. "I assume whoever locked me out of the house wanted to throw a wrench into my investigation, but it had the opposite effect. I know where Patrick is now."

Natalie's eyes widened in surprise. "Where?"

"In the cellar," Sarah replied.

Finn shook his head. "The cold must have affected your thinking, Sarah. We've already searched the cellar, remember?"

"I remember very well. I saw only two windows when we searched the cellar on Saturday. When I was outside this morning, I saw three."

"That's because there are three windows on that west wall," Vonnie said. "There always have been."

"On the outside," Sarah told her. "But Patrick must have changed the inside since you left. I think part of the cellar is walled off and that's where Patrick is hidden."

Levi rose slowly to his feet. "Then we'd better go find him."

She glanced at Amy and Audrey as everyone started to head out of the parlor. "I'm not sure we should all go. We don't know exactly what we're going to find down there."

She didn't want to think the worst, but there had been a lot of blood on the parlor floor and two full days had passed since Patrick's disappearance. If he was down there, he was either so injured he couldn't call for help or...worse.

Amy stepped forward. "We're going down there, Grandma," she said firmly. "You can't make us stay up here after everything we've been through."

"That's right," Audrey agreed, tugging on the hem of her fuzzy pink sweatshirt. "I'll stay toward the back because I don't want to see anything gross, but you can't just leave us up here."

The ten of them headed for the cellar with Sarah leading the way. Her feet still hurt from her trek out in the snow, but she ignored the pain. Finding Patrick was more important right now.

When they reached the cellar door, Sarah used the key to open the padlock and pulled open the steel door, the rest of them right behind her.

When she reached the bottom of the stairs, she looked around the large cellar, trying to orient herself. From the outside of the inn, the cellar windows had been evenly spaced about twelve feet apart.

She pointed toward the corner, where the west wall met the south wall. A plastic shelf unit stood in front of the wall. "He's got to be over there."

Without waiting for anyone to agree with her, Sarah rushed over to that corner and began tossing items off the shelves, mostly empty boxes. The others joined her, everyone but Natalie, who had her hands full with Bella.

"Patrick?" Levi called out. "Patrick, can you hear me?"

There was no answer. Sarah tried not to imagine the worst. She wouldn't let herself believe they'd come this far only to be disappointed once more.

Once the shelves were cleared, Sarah easily moved the shelf unit away from the wall, the plastic scraping against the cement floor. The sound made Bella start to cry, which provoked a coughing fit.

Sarah let Natalie tend to her child as she surveyed the long gray wall in front of them. Nothing about it screamed secret room, but Sarah knew there could be no other explanation for the window discrepancy.

Sarah walked up to the wall, searching for a seam or crack. "Does anyone see an opening?"

"Here," Vonnie called out. She stood near the corner where the two walls met. "I think I see a crack." She pushed on it and a panel in the wall swung open.

Sarah's breath caught in her throat when she saw it. The panel had been invisible to her before, but now it revealed an open doorway.

The small, cramped room behind the secret door was dark and chilly, the cellar window so dirty that no light showed through it. A damp, moldy odor invaded her nostrils and she heard Amy sneeze twice behind her.

"God bless you," Natalie whispered.

"Thanks," Amy whispered back.

When Sarah's eyes adjusted to the darkness she slowly scanned the room, realizing that Patrick wasn't there. Then she noticed a pile of old blankets in the corner.

And the pile was moving.

"There he is," she said, rushing toward the corner. Patrick lay on the cement floor, an open sleeping bag below him and a green army blanket pulled up to his forehead. A dirty blindfold covered his eyes and there was a gag over his dry, cracked mouth.

She gently pulled the blindfold off first, careful not to disturb the crude bandage covering his head. Then she removed the gag.

Patrick tried to speak, but no words came out of his swollen lips. Then he began to cough, the movement shaking his weak body. His cheeks were pale and drawn and his green eyes bloodshot.

"Someone get a glass of water," Sarah directed, placing a comforting hand on his shoulder. Relief shot through her that they'd found him alive. "You're going to be all right, Patrick. Don't try to talk right now."

Relief shone in his green eyes. He reached over and squeezed her hand, his grip so weak she barely felt the pressure of his fingers.

Vonnie returned with a glass of water and helped Patrick tilt his head up just far enough to take a sip. "Not too much," she warned, easing the glass toward his chapped lips. "You need to take it easy at first."

Patrick took two tiny sips of water and lay his head back down on the filthy blankets beneath him as if the exertion had exhausted him.

Levi brought a flashlight into the secret room, illuminating it for them. The eight-by-ten area was full of dust and cobwebs. For the first time, Sarah noticed that Patrick's left ankle was tethered to a metal pipe that ran from the floor to the ceiling, the orange rope too short to allow Patrick to reach the door.

"Who did this to you?" Sarah asked, but Patrick's eyes were closed and she couldn't be certain he was conscious.

She looked at the three men behind her. "We have to get him upstairs."

"Let me look him over first," Vonnie said. "Just to be sure it's safe to move him."

Sarah watched as Vonnie carefully checked his neck, back, and legs. Patrick winced as she moved his limbs and emitted a low moan every once in a while, but he didn't open his eyes again.

Natalie clutched Levi's arm. "He's in pain."

"His body's stiff and sore from lying on this cold, hard floor for so long," Vonnie explained, "and he's very weak and dehydrated."

Finn, Chuck, and Levi surrounded Patrick. Levi pulled a pocket knife from his jeans and cut through the rope binding Patrick to the pipe. Then the men slowly lifted Patrick off the cellar floor, using the sleeping bag underneath him as a makeshift stretcher.

The innkeeper moaned again as they carried him out of the dank, secret room and up the stairs. The other women followed, but Sarah remained in the secret room with the twins by her side.

"What are you doing, Grandma?" Audrey asked.

"Just looking around." Levi had left the flashlight on the floor. Sarah picked it up and walked over to examine the rope. Only it wasn't like any rope she'd ever seen. Several strands of thin, orange plastic fiber had been braided together to form the unbreakable tether.

As she examined the pile of blankets Patrick had lain on, all the pieces started falling together. The tether. The letter. The scrapbooks. The money. The quilts. All of the clues she had found up to this point finally pointed to one person.

Sarah had solved the mystery.

CHAPTER TWENTY-FOUR

When Sarah and the girls entered the parlor, they saw Patrick lying on the settee and everyone gathered in a circle around him. A thermal blanket covered his body, but his face was still pale.

"How is he?"

"In and out of consciousness," Vonnie said. "The sooner we can get him to a hospital, the better. He'll probably need IV fluids to rehydrate."

Natalie stood the farthest away from her birth father, holding Bella in her arms and looking as if she was trying not to cry.

"But his pulse is stronger now compared to when we first found him. To tell you the truth, he's lucky to be alive." Vonnie tilted his head slightly to reveal the clump of bloody, black hair on the back.

"Looks like somebody ambushed him from behind," Finn said, looking over the wound.

"It sure does," Vonnie agreed.

Sarah wasn't surprised. The culprit needed to make sure Patrick was out of commission during the weekend. Although, she wondered now if that clanging sound they'd heard had been Patrick banging on the pipe. Perhaps he had found a tool of sorts to alert them to his presence.

Unfortunately, it hadn't worked.

"I wish he could tell us who put him down there," Levi said with a sigh.

"He doesn't have to," Sarah replied. "Because I know who did it."

Sarah moved to the center of the room, feeling every eye upon her. So much had happened since she'd been awakened this morning, but it was all suddenly so clear that she wondered why she hadn't seen it before.

"It took me until now to figure it all out," Sarah began.

No one said anything and she saw them cast nervous glances around the room.

"You mean it's really someone in this room?" Natalie said, her eyes wide. "One of us?"

Sarah nodded as she turned to Finn. "To be honest, you were on the top of everyone's suspect list including mine. That black eye made you look guilty, and the fact that you wore the same suit as the night before."

"I fell asleep going over some paperwork," Finn said. "It wasn't the first time I've slept in my clothes."

"Those facts," Sarah continued, "along with the way you treated everyone made it easy to picture you attacking Patrick and trying to get away with it."

Dorothy scooted away from him as Sarah continued. "Then there was the fact that you wanted to buy the inn. You knew about the government inspector's plan to cite the Red Clover Inn for safety violations. That gave you a major financial incentive to convince Patrick to sell, by whatever means necessary. Even if it meant sending him a threatening letter."

"My assistant wrote that letter," Finn said and cleared his throat. "She tends toward melodrama. I should have read the letter before I signed it, but I trusted her."

A flash of pain lit his eyes so quickly that Sarah almost missed it. Then they were dark pools of brown again, revealing nothing of the man beneath the surface.

"Then you told us that story about running into the door." Sarah shook her head. "Not very creative, Finn."

"The truth can be boring, but I figured a lie would be worse." Finn pulled a pack of cigarettes from his pocket, then seemed to remember where he was and put them back again. "You can all believe what you want, but I'm not the one who attacked Patrick."

Sarah glanced down at the unconscious innkeeper. "It's hard to convince people of your innocence when it looks like you've been in a brawl." Then she turned to Levi. "Or when you've spent time in prison. You've been at the top of my suspect list ever since I learned Patrick fired you Friday night."

Everyone but Natalie looked surprised by this revelation. Sarah assumed Levi must have already told her, having learned his lesson about keeping secrets.

"You slammed the door when you left that night," Sarah continued. "You knew losing your third job in a row would cause problems with your probation, so you figured you'd find a way to talk yourself back into Patrick's good graces in the morning."

Watching Levi's expression told Sarah she was right on the money, so she kept going. "You knew he'd been under a lot of stress, what with the leaky roof and Pittman pressing him for a bribe. You were hoping he'd give you a second chance. Only when you got here on Saturday morning, Patrick was missing, so you decided to just pretend he hadn't fired you."

Levi dug his hands into his pants pockets. "I didn't know what else to do. I couldn't just leave you all here to fend for yourselves."

"But that wasn't the only reason, was it?" Sarah said. "You never went back to Hartford that night."

"No." Levi shifted on his feet. "I was really upset about Patrick firing me, so I drove around for a while trying to think of ways to get my job back."

"And ran into the snowstorm?" Sarah said.

"No," he said, looking embarrassed. "My car slid on the ice and went into a ditch. It had already started snowing when I headed back toward the inn on foot. I barely made it back here—that much was true. But when I found out Patrick was missing, I knew it was my chance to step up and really prove myself to him."

"You weren't the only one who had something to prove." Her gaze landed on Natalie. "An unemployed single mother with a baby didn't seem like a typical guest you'd find at the Red Clover Inn. I knew there had to be another reason you were here, financial or...otherwise."

Vonnie spun around to look at Natalie. "What do you mean by financial?"

"I mean, money is always a motive," Sarah replied. "That's certainly true for you and Chuck. Did you all notice how Chuck and Vonnie were so helpful after Patrick disappeared? They made themselves right at home. I soon found out the inn had been their home years ago—and with Patrick gone, it could be again."

"You're accusing us?" Chuck asked incredulously.

"I did see you scuffling with Patrick the night he disappeared."

"You don't know what you saw," Chuck growled. "I was talking to Patrick about our room and it got a little heated, but then Patrick stumbled over the rug and fell on top of me."

The other guests stared at him until Chuck shifted in his seat. "Don't look at me like that. Vonnie and I are only here to get what's rightfully ours."

"That's right," Sarah said. "The money." Then she turned to Dorothy. "You might refer to it as loot."

Dorothy's hand fluttered to her throat. "I beg your pardon."

"I believe it was money you and your husband stole while on your honeymoon crime spree fifty years ago. I read newspaper articles in one of those scrapbooks about the British Bonnie and Clyde duo who were robbing banks up and down the East Coast, including a couple of banks in Hartford."

Vonnie blinked in surprise. "That was you?"

"Of course not," Dorothy said with a huff. "Do I sound British to you?" She rose stiffly to her feet. "If this is your idea of a joke, Sarah Hart, I don't think it's very funny. Leo and I did no such thing. How dare you besmirch his memory!"

"It's no joke," Sarah told her. "You're the one who attacked Patrick and locked him in the cellar. You also falsely accused me of attacking you and lured me outside this morning to keep me from finding out the truth. Only it backfired on you. If I hadn't been locked outside, I might never have figured it out."

Sarah could see everyone looking at her like she was crazy. Seventy-two-year-old Dorothy Ogden looked so frail standing there in her blood-stained robe. That's why she had always hovered near the bottom of Sarah's suspect list. No one could imagine Dorothy overpowering a man like Patrick.

"I'm afraid your detective skills leave a lot to be desired," Dorothy held up her hands. "I have arthritis. I could never do all the things you've accused me of. I certainly couldn't carry a grown man down those cellar stairs."

"No, but you probably could manage to drag him from the parlor and down the stairs on a quilt." She walked over to the front desk and retrieved the quilt she had placed behind it. "This quilt, to be exact." She unfurled it over the wood floor, revealing the blood stains soaked into the fabrics. "It's one of my favorite patterns called Flower Basket. As soon as I saw it in that secret room in the cellar, I knew for sure you were Patrick's attacker."

"Ridiculous," sputtered Dorothy.

"Not when each guest room here has a theme with a bed quilt to match. All of them were perfect: Bear Claw in the twins' wilderness-style room, Log Cabin in Levi's pioneer-style room. Natalie had a Flying Geese quilt in her bird-themed room and Finn had a Railroad Crossing quilt in his train-themed room. The quilt in my room honored Patrick's grandmother. Only your quilt seemed out of sync with your room's theme."

"I had the Evening Star quilt," Dorothy said, "that can go with anything."

"You're right," Sarah replied. "That's why it didn't match your room. It's too generic for a garden-themed room. It certainly doesn't go as well as this Flower Basket quilt would."

Finn's brow furrowed. "What are you saying?"

"I'm saying that Patrick must have caught Dorothy looking for the stolen loot she and her husband had left behind fifty years ago. He probably threatened to throw her out. That's when she hit him from behind with something heavy—maybe even that fireplace poker over there. He's lucky she has arthritis or the blow might have killed him. Only she didn't realize there'd be so much blood. She got the quilt off her bed and used it to try and clean up the mess. That's when she must have noticed Patrick was still alive. Lucky for him, she just wanted him out of the way for a while, not dead."

"I'm not sure a jury will make that distinction," Finn said.

Dorothy bristled. "I don't have to sit here and listen to this." She sprang for the door, moving with the speed of a woman half her age.

"Grab her," Sarah shouted.

Levi jumped in front of her, blocking her path while Chuck caught up with her from behind. He snagged her elbow. "You're not going anywhere yet, lady."

"This is preposterous," Dorothy cried. "She's accusing me of a serious crime on the basis of a quilt pattern? That will never stand up in court."

"I think it will when combined with the other evidence," Sarah said confidently.

Dorothy blanched. "What other evidence?"

"The fact that fifty years ago a young couple was robbing small banks and savings-and-loans up and down the East Coast. According to the witnesses, only the woman did the talking and she had a pronounced British accent."

"Which I obviously do not," Dorothy stated.

"Not anymore," Sarah agreed. "You've had over forty years to get rid of your accent, but some things are too ingrained in us to change, especially when we're under stress."

"Like what?" Natalie asked.

"Spelling." Sarah pulled the anonymous letter she had received from her pocket. "I read this too fast the first time to notice the discrepancy, but you spelled *license* the British way, with a C instead of an S."

Dorothy didn't blink. "Since I didn't type that letter, I didn't misspell anything."

"How did you know it was typed?" Sarah asked, turning the letter around for everyone to see. "I never mentioned that. Patrick's printer doesn't work. The only way for someone to type this letter was to do it on the old Smith-Corona that was up in the attic."

The color drained from Dorothy's face.

"Even if she typed that letter," Chuck said. "How could she possibly have caught Patrick so off guard?"

"I think she drugged him," Sarah explained. "He was drinking a can of soda when I arrived Friday night and I remember wondering if he'd spiked it. His behavior seemed a little odd to me. Then you said he stumbled and fell during your argument."

"That's right," Chuck said thoughtfully. "I thought he was a little tipsy too."

"If he was inebriated that night," Dorothy said, "perhaps Patrick did this to himself and decided to sleep it off in his secret room."

"Where he gagged and blindfolded himself," Finn said wryly, "and tethered himself to an iron pipe?"

Dorothy sagged against Chuck.

"She has those little white pills," Sarah reminded the group. "She gave one of them to Natalie yesterday afternoon to calm her down."

"It knocked me out," Natalie said. "And I felt groggy for hours afterward."

"She's been sedating him all weekend," Sarah told them. "She couldn't take a chance that he would try to signal us, like clanging on that iron pipe."

"That was him?" Levi exclaimed. "I thought it was the plumbing acting up again."

"And Dorothy planted that seed," Sarah said. "She had to reveal one of her secrets to do it though, letting us know she'd stayed at the inn fifty years ago."

"And you consider that solid evidence of my guilt?" Dorothy sputtered. "I didn't do it."

"Yes," Patrick rasped from the settee. "You did."

Sarah had been so caught up in revealing all her clues that she hadn't noticed he'd regained consciousness.

"Sarah is right...about everything." Patrick licked his lips as he struggled to sit up. "That Flower Basket quilt was on her bed when she checked in. The next evening, I found Dorothy pulling up floor boards in the parlor. When I told her to leave the inn, she agreed. Then everything went black." He paused to take a deep breath. "The next thing I knew I was in the cellar."

Vonnie moved to his side. "Don't talk too much, Patrick. You'll wear yourself out."

"No," he replied, "let me finish. I wasn't sure if I'd ever get the chance to say the things I need to say." Then he turned to Natalie. "I knew you were my daughter the moment you walked into the inn. You have my grandmother's eyes."

"Then why didn't you say anything?" Natalie asked him.

He looked away. "I wasn't sure why you'd come here. The last time I heard from your mother was when she wrote to me just before your eighteenth birthday, demanding what I owed her in back child support. I thought maybe you were here to collect money I didn't have to give."

Sarah watched the play of emotions on Natalie's face, not certain what the girl was thinking.

Patrick leaned further back against the pillows, signs of fatigue starting to set in.

Natalie stepped toward him. "You really thought I just wanted your money?" Tears gleamed in her eyes. "You're my father. You're the only family Bella and I have left." She reached out her hand to him and Patrick took it.

"It's not too late," he said.

Natalie shook her head. "No. It's never too late."

Dorothy wriggled her arm, trying to free herself from Chuck's grasp. "I still say there's no solid evidence against me. Poor Patrick's suffered a head injury and been drugged. He's doesn't know what he's saying."

Sarah pulled the orange rope from her bag. "I call this solid evidence." It was the rope that had been used to tie Patrick to the pipe. "While the men were carrying Patrick upstairs, I took a close look at it. Someone made it by braiding several strands of orange jelly yarn together. I recognized it because my friend Martha has used jelly yarn just like this to crochet beach bags for her grandkids."

Sarah pointed to the knitting basket by the window. "I believe we'll find that same orange yarn in Dorothy's basket."

Dorothy made a move toward it, but Chuck grabbed her arm to stop her. Levi retrieved the basket and brought it back to the group. He tossed several balls of yarn out of the basket until he pulled out a hank of orange jelly yarn.

It was a perfect match to the makeshift rope.

"I don't believe it," Finn breathed.

CHAPTER TWENTY-FIVE

onnie tore the bloody Flower Basket quilt out of Sarah's grasp before anyone could stop her and turned to Chuck.

"This is it. This is the basket mother was talking about." Vonnie looked at her husband, her eyes shining with happy tears. "I knew there was a Flower Basket quilt somewhere in this place and we finally have it!"

He stepped toward her, his beefy hand still encircling Dorothy's wrist. "Are you sure?"

Vonnie held the quilt open in front of her, studying the colorful pattern beneath the blood stain. "It has to be. We've looked in every other basket in this place."

"Your mother always did have a strange sense of humor," Chuck said.

Now Sarah understood another piece of the puzzle. "So that's why you reserved the room with the garden theme," she said to the Thayers, "and why you were so angry when Patrick gave it to Dorothy."

"No offense," Finn said, studying the blood-stained quilt in Vonnie's hands. "But that quilt doesn't look all that impressive to me. I doubt it's worth much now that Patrick's bled all over it."

"That's where you're wrong," Vonnie replied and, before anyone could move, she stuck her fingers between some loose threads and ripped the quilt open.

The sound of tearing fabric made Sarah take a sharp breath, but it was too late to stop Vonnie. She ripped the top of the quilt open and laughed as dozens of hundred dollar bills spilled out of the fabric and onto the floor.

"Wow." Levi whistled low. "That's a lot of dough."

Vonnie kept ripping the quilt, almost in a frenzy now, as Chuck let go of Dorothy and began scooping up the money on the floor.

Dorothy tried to push him aside. "That's my money. Leave it alone."

Vonnie's head jerked up. "Yours? Mother hid this treasure for us."

An angry flush suffused Dorothy's powdered cheeks. "The only reason she had it in the first place is because she threatened to turn us in to the police. It was hush money. And I've come to take it back."

Finn clasped his hands behind his head as he leaned back in his chair. "I guess you never imagined it would be sewn into a quilt."

"Obviously not," Dorothy said.

"That explains why we kept hearing noises in the night," Sarah told the other guests. "Dorothy got Patrick out of the way so she could search the inn without interference. She assumed once he was missing, we'd all leave. But Mother Nature foiled her plans and trapped us all here together."

Vonnie stepped toward Dorothy. "You played the sweet old lady when you were really a viper in disguise."

"Look in the mirror, honey," Dorothy said, dropping her mask of civility. "You've been searching this place from stem to stern. I saw you sneaking around at night, trying to steal what's mine."

Finn started laughing. "It was yours, all right," he told Dorothy. "You went to all that trouble to find your money and it was in the quilt right on top of your bed."

The rumble of an engine drew Levi to the parlor window. "The snowplows are out. The roads will be clear soon."

Sarah breathed a silent prayer of thanks. She had nabbed the guilty party just in time. Now she couldn't wait to get back to Maple Hill.

"See if the phone is working yet," Chuck suggested. "We need to call the police."

Dorothy walked over to the wing chair and sat down. "Yes, we do. That money is rightfully mine. The statute of limitations ran out on those robberies long ago. Otherwise, I never would have come back here."

"But you're still guilty of assaulting Patrick and kidnapping him," Sarah reminded her.

Dorothy sank back in her chair, pulling the collar of her robe together. "But I'm just a feeble old woman. I didn't know what I was doing. My mind isn't what it used to be."

"Save it for the jury," Finn said. "We're not buying it."

Sarah looked at all the money littering the floor, amazed at how much trouble it had caused. Vonnie had just referred to it as a treasure. She remembered the verse Maeve Maguire had written in her Bible.

"Do not store up for yourselves treasures on earth," Sarah murmured to herself, "where moth and rust destroy, and where thieves break in and steal. But store up for yourselves treasures in heaven, where moth and rust do not destroy, and where thieves do not break in and steal. For where your treasure is, there your heart will be also."

"Did you say something, Grandma?" Audrey asked her.

"Yes," Sarah replied, circling an arm around each of her granddaughters. That Bible verse was a lesson she definitely wanted to share with them. "I'll tell you all about it when we go upstairs to pack. It's time to go home."

CHAPTER TWENTY-SIX

S arah carried her suitcase downstairs in time to see the paramedics hang the portable IV above a stretcher set up in the parlor. The twins were still upstairs, taking a few last pictures of their unusual room.

"I'm not going to any hospital," Patrick announced from his spot on the settee. "I'm perfectly fine."

Natalie and Levi stood on either side of him. "I think you should go," Natalie said. "Levi can hold down the fort here. He did a great job while you were missing."

Patrick cast a skeptical glance up at Levi. "No joke?" Then his brow furrowed. "Why do I remember you shouting my name?"

"When we finally found the spare key to the cellar, we searched for you there," Levi told him. "I thought for sure we'd find you. I didn't know about the secret room."

"That's because it was supposed to be a secret. I only told Dorothy about it because she seemed like such a sweet old lady. I thought she might get a kick out of it."

Finn trotted down the stairs with a garment bag slung over one shoulder. "That will teach you not to trust sweet old ladies," he told Patrick.

"Well, I think you can trust Levi," Natalie told Patrick. "So why don't you go to the hospital and get checked out? For your daughter's—and your granddaughter's—sake."

Sarah smiled to herself. Natalie had played the trump card and from the expression on Patrick's face, he knew it.

"Fine," he grumbled. "I'll go to the hospital."

The paramedics prepared to move Patrick to the stretcher while Natalie turned to Finn. "I guess you're leaving."

"Not soon enough, I'm sure," Finn said. "But I will give you one piece of advice before I go. Be careful. Mr. Prince over there still might turn out to be a real toad."

Despite her defense of Levi, Sarah could see that Natalie still wasn't quite sure about him. That was a good thing, in Sarah's opinion. Natalie was too young to put her trust in someone so soon. Trust had to be earned over time, especially since she had a young child to care for.

Sarah looked over at the alcove where Chuck and Vonnie sat speaking to a detective. The police had hauled Dorothy off when they'd first arrived at the inn and were now taking witness statements. Sarah had already given hers, basically going over the same information she had revealed when proving her case against Dorothy.

She couldn't hear what the detective was saying to the Thayers, but Vonnie was very animated, waving her hands in the air and talking almost nonstop. Chuck sat beside her, rubbing his knee and steadily nodding his head while his wife spoke.

Finn walked up to Sarah. "I guess this is good-bye. If I ever have a mystery to solve, you'll be the first one I call."

"Thanks," Sarah said with a smile. "I think."

He held out his hand. "It's been a pleasure."

She shook his hand. "I'm not sure that's a word I'd use to describe this weekend, but it's definitely been an experience."

Finn chuckled. "It has at that. One I never want to repeat."

"Agreed." She waved good-bye to him as he walked out of the inn.

"Can you believe it?" Vonnie exclaimed as she and Chuck emerged from of the alcove. "I think we should call our lawyer right now."

"We can't afford a lawyer, hon," Chuck said wearily.

Sarah turned to them. "Is something wrong?"

"That detective over there said the money doesn't belong to us. He said something about possession being nine-tenths of the law and some other legal mumbo jumbo. I took down his badge number. You can bet his superiors are going to hear about this!"

"So what happens to the money?" Sarah asked, suspecting she already knew.

"Patrick gets all of it," Chuck replied. "Every single hundred dollar bill. Can you believe it? He didn't even know that money was here."

"It's a travesty," Vonnie muttered as she headed for the front door. "A travesty, I tell you."

"Looks like we're leaving," Chuck said, following his wife. "Bye, Sarah."

"Bye."

She moved toward the stairs to tell the twins it was time to go when Natalie and Levi intercepted her.

"Thanks for everything," Natalie said, cuddling her baby in her arms. "I mean, helping me with Bella and stuff. I really appreciate it."

"You're welcome. I was happy to do it." She turned to Levi. "Do you think Patrick will let you keep your job?" she asked him.

Levi nodded. "He said he'll give me one more chance. I'm determined not to blow it this time."

Sarah reached out to shake his hand. "Good-bye, Levi."

"Bye, Sarah," Natalie said, giving her an awkward hug, the baby sandwiched between them.

"Good-bye, you two." She kissed the top of Bella's head and squeezed Natalie's shoulder. "I think you're going to be a great mom."

"Thanks," Natalie said softly. "I think Bella and I are going to stay on here for a while. Patrick invited us."

Sarah knew that didn't make them an instant family, but at least father and daughter would have a chance to get to know each other. Building relationships took time. And Bella would gain a grandfather. In her opinion, children could never have too many people who loved them in their lives.

"Hey, Sarah," Patrick called out as the paramedics began wheeling him toward the door. "Next time you're in Hartford, you get a free night's stay at the Red Clover."

"Thank you," she called after him, not sure she ever wanted to come back. The only place she wanted to be at this moment was Maple Hill.

They left the Red Clover Inn shortly after noon. As soon as their cell phone reception resumed, the twins called their parents and gave them an abbreviated report of their harrowing weekend, promising full details when they arrived home.

Sarah tried to call Martha but kept getting a busy signal. Jason and Maggie assured her that William was all right and there was no emergency as far as they knew, but she still felt uneasy. She couldn't remember the last time she had gone four days without talking to her best friend.

"I never thought I'd be so happy to see Maple Hill," Audrey said with a sigh. "Wait until we tell everybody at school about what happened to us."

"I'm going to write it all down for my English assignment," Amy said. "Mrs. Coopersmith wants us to tell a nonfiction story, but she probably won't believe all of it really happened!"

Sarah could hardly believe it herself. Her adrenalin was still pumping from solving the mystery at the last moment, but she knew she'd be dragging tomorrow. She planned to take a few days to rest and catch up on visits with her father and friends, then start to work on restoring some of those tattered, vintage quilts Patrick had sent home with her.

But right now, the only thing she wanted to do was soak in a hot bubble bath. Every muscle in her body ached from all the hard work of breaking into the screened porch this morning, and a nice long bath would soothe her sore muscles.

Something told her the Thayers wouldn't get over the pain of losing Vonnie's mother's ill-gotten rainy-day fund quite so easily.

"We're nearly there," Amy said, sounding almost giddy as Sarah turned onto Bristol Street.

"I just want to tell you girls again how proud I am of both of you," Sarah said. "We had a rough weekend, but we made it through."

"Yeah," Audrey said, "but next time you want to take us on vacation can we just go to Disney World or something?"

Sarah smiled. "Sounds good to me."

Jason and Maggie emerged from their rambling Victorian house as soon as Sarah pulled her car into their driveway. The girls jumped out and raced to their parents, the four of them exchanging hugs all around.

By the time Sarah climbed out of the car, Jason was at the driver's door to meet her. "Hey, Mom," he said, pulling her in for a hug. "Sounds like you three had quite a weekend."

"We sure did."

"We knew they'd gotten a lot of snow down that way," Jason said as they joined Maggie and the girls on the front walk, "but we had no idea you were snowbound."

"I'm glad I didn't know," Maggie said, "I would have gone crazy with worry." She held open the front door for Sarah. "I hope you can stay for some tomato soup and grilled cheese sandwiches. We want to hear every detail about what happened this weekend."

Sarah's stomach had been growling for the last fifty miles. They'd been so anxious to get home that they'd decided not to stop for lunch. "That sounds wonderful."

A car horn sounded just as Sarah was about to step through the door. She turned around to see Martha's car pulling up to the curb.

"I'll be right in," Sarah promised, ready to find out why her best friend had been texting urgent messages to her all weekend.

Martha emerged from the driver's seat wearing a brown wool coat and a wide smile. "I was just on my way to your house when I saw your car in the driveway. I've been trying to reach you all weekend."

"I know." Sarah rounded the front of her car. "I didn't have cell phone reception, but I kept getting your texts. Was something wrong? You had me worried sick."

"Oh no!" Martha started laughing until she doubled over. She placed a hand over her stomach as she straightened. "Oh, Sarah, I'm sorry. I didn't mean to make you worry. I did have an important message for you, though."

Sarah relaxed, certain it couldn't be bad news if Martha was laughing like that. "What is it?"

"The grocery store was having a weekend special on fresh organic pineapples." Martha grinned. "I know how much you like them, so I thought you might want me to pick some up for you."

"Pineapples?" Sarah said, a giggle bubbling up in her throat. After all the tension of the last few days, it felt so good to laugh again. "All those urgent texts were about pineapples?"

"That's right." Martha said. "I didn't want you to miss the sale, so when you didn't get back to me I bought some for you anyway. I was just heading over to your house to drop them off."

Sarah spied the fresh pineapples sitting in a box in Martha's backseat and started craving pineapple upside-down cake. "How much do I owe you?"

"A cup of coffee at Liam's should do it," Martha replied. "Your treat."

"Deal." Sarah reached out to give her a hug, so grateful to be home among her special treasures once again.

About the Author

Kristin Eckhardt is the author of more than thirty books, including eight books for Guideposts' Mysteries of Sparrow Island and Home to Heather Creek series. She's won two national awards for her writing and her first book was made into a television movie. Kristin and her husband raised three children on their farm in central Nebraska and are active in their church and community.

CHAPTER ONE

*A*ntoinette held her breath. Someone was coming in. If she were to be discovered here, she would be the next to die. Light from the hall played across pale hair. It was the murderer. It was—

"Sarah? Are you home?"

Sarah Hart nearly jumped out of her rocking chair. She looked toward the partially open front door, her eyes wide. Cold night air blew in, the March chill sneaking beneath the lap quilt that covered her legs. For a moment, she couldn't pull herself out of the mystery she'd been reading.

"Sarah?" asked the same voice again.

Sarah stood and pushed her reading glasses up on her head, sweeping back the short curtain of her graying blonde hair. Ella Buttonwood hobbled into the living room, all four feet, eleven-and-a-half inches of her. Her silky white hair and unsteady gait made Ella look fragile, but Sarah knew better. Not only did Ella run her diner with stern efficiency, but she moderated Maple Hill town meetings without blinking an eye.

"Ella, you startled me!" Sarah set the book on the rocking chair her late husband Gerry had made for her.

"I'm sorry, Sarah. I knocked twice, but when you didn't answer I peeked in and saw a light on. The door was open, so I thought I'd see if you were home."

"Of course! I must have been so caught up in my novel I didn't hear you knocking." It was a normal occurrence for Sarah's friends and family to just walk into the house if the door was open, but Sarah was a bit surprised to see Ella walk in. They were friendly enough when they ran into each other in town, but they didn't spend much time together. "What brings you out here so late?"

"I'm sorry, but I heard you're going to Texas tomorrow, and I had to see you before you left," Ella said.

"Yes, I'm going to visit my daughter and her family."

"I just need you to look at it before you leave. Will you? I left it right outside the door on the porch."

"It?" Sarah's curiosity was piqued.

"The proof I've been searching for my whole life. Proof that my grandmother's stories about our house being a station on the Underground Railroad are true."

"Maybe you'd better start at the beginning, Ella." They both sat on the couch, knees angled toward each other. It seemed odd to see Ella without the apron she always had on at the Miss Maple, the diner she ran. Tonight, her knobby gray sweater nearly reached the knees of her khaki slacks.

"Remember last spring when everyone got water in their cellars?" Ella asked.

"Of course. Between all the rain and melting snow, I thought we'd need canoes."

"My whole cellar flooded last year. Not that I went down to check because, with this bum knee, steps are more difficult for me with every passing year. I haven't been down in the cellar in ages. We've got water again this year."

"I'm sorry. It's such a mess!"

"Actually it's been a blessing in disguise. While my nephew was cleaning up, he noticed a section of the foundation wall had begun to crumble. It must have been weakened by last year's flood, and the water this year was too much for it."

"And *that* was a blessing?" Sarah asked.

Ella laughed. "Yes. Though I don't know what I'd do without my nephew and niece. Ryan and his sister Chelsea were able to take down that section of the wall to see what repairs we'd have to make."

Sarah nodded. Ella had never married, but for the past six or seven years, she had been the guardian of her younger sister's children. Ella's sister and her husband had died in an automobile accident. The children, now teenagers, had survived and had come to live with Ella.

"And guess what we found once the wall was down?"

"I have no idea," Sarah said.

Ella stood up and took Sarah's arm as if Sarah were a child. "Come and see!"

Sarah tightened the tie on her thick bathrobe and went with Ella to the front entry. Ella opened the front door, careful not to let the wind catch the door and swing it wildly.

"Here it is," Ella said as she picked up a black garbage bag and brought it inside. It looked full. "My proof, or at least one part of it."

"What is it?" Sarah asked as she firmly shut the front door. The wind howled against the house.

Ella started to untie the top of the bag, then hesitated. "Is there anyone else here?"

Sarah shook her head. "Just us."

"Good! I don't want everyone knowing about this until you confirm it is what I think it is." Ella started walking toward the dining room. "Is it okay if I put it on your table? It won't hurt it, I promise."

"I suppose so."

Curious, Sarah turned on the overhead light. The prisms on the brass chandelier glistened brightly on the long table and the fireplace at one side of the room. She gathered up some quilting books that she'd left on the table earlier and set them in the bookcase by the door. Then she turned to watch Ella carry the bag to the table.

Whatever was in the bag must not be too heavy. Ella swung it up onto the table with ease. And it had to be soft since Sarah didn't hear any thunk.

Ella opened the bag and drew out a quilt, gently spreading it across the table. It wasn't large, no bigger than would cover a twin bed. The colors were mostly dark and subdued, except for one garish red fabric. Each quilt block was made up of concentric squares, a series of squares one within another. Each section of the squares was very narrow.

Sarah's nose wrinkled at the odor of mildew. It wasn't unusual with old quilts, but it warned that the quilt might need a lot of restoration work.

"You think this quilt is proof that your house was a stop on the Underground Railroad?" Sarah asked.

"It could be, if it's the right age." Ella looked at her hopefully. "What do you think?"

"Do you have any idea how long the wall was up?" Sarah set her reading glasses in place again. They were good enough for a quick examination. She would need to get her magnifying glass from the sewing room to do more. She slowly walked around the long table so she could view the quilt from every angle.

"A long time. I was born in that house, and nobody's ever mentioned who built that wall. This quilt must be really old, right?" Ella trailed around the table after Sarah, matching each of her steps.

"I'd need a few days and much better light to tell you that." She looked up at Ella who was appraising her as closely as Sarah was the quilt.

Sarah continued to examine the quilt, running her fingers along the fabric and the seams. She squeezed one section, then several others.

"What are you doing?" Ella asked.

"I'm trying to see what's underneath the quilt's top layer."

"With your fingers?"

"Yes." She pointed at the quilt. "Squeeze it."

"Where?"

Sarah smiled. "Anywhere. It's a way of gauging the resistance in the quilt's layers. That tells me what sort of batting might have been used."

Ella pinched the quilt. "I'm not sure what I'm looking for. What's it supposed to feel like?"

"This quilt feels a bit spongy. It doesn't have the sturdiness of a modern quilt sewn with cotton batting. Some areas are thicker than others, which could mean there's an even older quilt in the middle."

"Really? Would that quilt be more valuable?"

"Not necessarily." Sarah said. "When an old quilt is used for batting, it's usually because it's too worn for any other use. Collectors want well-preserved quilts. I could open up a seam and look at what's inside and—"

"No!" Ella shook her head in horror. "You can't rip up an antique quilt. You'd ruin it."

"I know how to do it without damaging the quilt."

"I don't want to risk it."

"Don't worry." Sarah leaned closer to look at the ties scattered through the quilt. "I wouldn't do anything to the quilt without your permission."

"I don't want the quilt damaged." Once Ella got an idea lodged in her head, she never let it go, no matter how many logical reasons anyone gave. She'd been that way since Sarah first met her in grade school.

Sarah kept looking at the quilt, ignoring Ella's hand pressed protectively on it. "The strips of fabric that create the squares are very narrow."

"Does that mean something? What about the pattern?"

"Antique quilts are often made from thin strips of fabric because material was hard to come by in the nineteenth century and earlier. This is a variation on the Log Cabin pattern, which became popular in the United States around the time of the Civil War."

"But this quilt could have been put together before the Civil War, couldn't it?" Ella asked.

"Yes, it could be an antebellum quilt." Sarah picked up one corner to get a good view of the stitching.

Ella's pressure on the quilt lessened slightly. "Do you think it could have belonged to a runaway slave?"

Sarah paused. "Why do you think it belonged to a slave?"

"Someone closed up a break in the real foundation long ago." Ella said. "We can see that a different stone was used. Maybe that was why the false wall was put up in the first place. To hide that there'd been a hole there. If my grandmother was right, that opening was connected to a hiding place for runaway slaves."

"Wow! Wouldn't that be something?"

Ella nodded, her smile broadening. "Once I know for sure that my cellar was a station, I want to open a museum. Nothing big or fancy. A couple of exhibit spaces in the cellar. School kids can come and see what slaves endured in their flight to freedom. It's what Maple Hill needs. Stockbridge may have Alice's Restaurant and the Norman Rockwell Museum, but we'll have the Maple Hill Underground Railroad Center. I've already contacted a couple of experts to come look at the house and give me their opinions."

"That would be a wonderful thing for Maple Hill," Sarah said. "But I can't be certain that this quilt is old enough to fit that time period until I look at it more closely. There are a lot of things I need to check. Would you be willing to leave it here so I can look at it when I get back from Texas?"

Ella shook her head. "I need to show it to the experts tomorrow."

"They're coming so soon?"

"If the house is truly a previously unknown Underground Railroad site, it's a major find." She began to stuff the quilt into the garbage bag.

Sarah winced and reached out a hand to halt her. "Do you mind if I take some photos of it?"

"Go ahead if it'll help you."

Ella smoothed the quilt out on the table while Sarah got her camera. Sarah retraced her steps around the table, taking a dozen shots of the quilt's pattern and stitching. She turned the quilt over and snapped as many of the bottom. A quick check of the photos told her that she could see the details of the pattern and the stitching. She put the camera on the fireplace mantel.

"Those will really help, Ella," Sarah said. "I'm glad you brought it over."

"Now you can see why I couldn't wait to show this to you." Ella began to roll up the quilt.

"I'll need to spend a lot more time checking out the stitching and the knots and the fabric. Then I'll need to compare it to already dated quilts. After that, I should be able to put an approximate date on your quilt."

Ella tied the bag closed. "But you think it's old, and that's enough for me right now."

"When can you bring it back so I can get to work on dating it more accurately?"

"I'm not sure. I can't promise anything until I know what's going on. I've contacted the Elijah Burt House in Longmeadow and the Seth Hunt House in Northampton. They're both Underground Railroad sites, and they're both sending out someone to look at my house. They're almost as excited as I am." She chuckled. "If that's possible."

Sarah walked with Ella into the foyer. Ella reached for the door, and Sarah wrapped her arms around herself. Even her thick robe wouldn't stop that icy wind. "I hope they can confirm your house as a station. It'd be such a great thing for Maple Hill and for your family."

Ella smiled and opened the front door. "I'll let them know what you've told me about the quilt."

"I can't wait to go over it in detail. I'm sure it's got lots of secrets to share with us."

A Note from the Editors

Guideposts, a nonprofit organization, touches millions of lives every day through products and services that inspire, encourage and uplift. Our magazines, books, prayer network and outreach programs help people connect their faith-filled values to their daily lives. To learn more, visit www.guideposts. com or www.guidepostsfoundation.org.